READY WHEN YOU ARE

READY WHEN YOU ARE

YOU ARE

GARY LONESBOROUGH

Library of Congress Cataloging-in-Publication Data available

ISBN 978-1-338-74954-0

1 2021

Printed in the U.S.A. 23
First edition, February 2022

Book design by Christopher Stengel

CY 11 02 2021 0338

For
Mum and Dad

ONE

The white boys stare at us from the pub. It's Ethan and his mates. They sit on stools behind the railing of the packed pub and sip their beers from schooner glasses, keeping their eyes on us. Next to me, Kalyn stares back at them from behind the steering wheel, his mouth tucked at one corner and his eyebrows scrunched, while Jarny lights a cigarette in the back seat.

"What you bastards lookin' at?" Jarny shouts. They just stare, then they laugh. And I just look to my lap, because there's a cop car facing us, stopped on the other side of this red light. I know they're watching us—the pickup with all the black faces inside. My throat is drying, but I don't want to drink from my bottle of Coke, in case the coppers think it's a beer and pull us over.

The white boys go back to their drinks and banter as the light turns green and Kalyn eases off the brakes. I expect him to put his foot to the floor and spin the tires, but he must spot the coppers too. We drive steadily past them, blasting our music, and start up the mountain out of town. In the side-view mirror I see the police car slow, then spin around. Now they're coming, speeding up behind us. It's Constable Rogers driving. I'd recognize those big ears of his anywhere.

"No sudden movements, lads," Kalyn jokes as he watches the rearview mirror. Jarny ashes his cigarette on the interior armrest of the door. The cops' lights come on and spray red and blue into the car. Kalyn flicks on his blinker with a sigh and pulls over. My heart is pounding.

The doors of the police car open as Kalyn turns off the engine. Constable Rogers comes to Kalyn's window with his breathalyzer in hand. He peeks inside.

"Kalyn, Jackson, and Jarny," he says, with such dissatisfaction. "What are you boys doing? Mouthing off at the fellas in the pub?"

"Nah," Kalyn tells him. "Just saying hello."

"Is that right?" Constable Rogers says, his voice dropping an octave. "Seemed a bit to me like youse were trying to start trouble."

"Nope. No trouble," Kalyn replies.

The other copper approaches my side of the truck, red-faced, walking slow, eyes searching through the open windows until he stops by me, staring me down. Constable Rogers holds up his breathalyzer to Kalyn. Kalyn breathes into it before the breathalyzer beeps.

"Looks like you're all good."

I feel such a relief come over my body, even though I know Kalyn hasn't been drinking.

"Have a safe drive, boys."

The coppers walk back to their car. Kalyn starts the truck and we're back on the road.

"Turn it up," Jarny shouts, as "Hypnotize" by Biggie Smalls starts through the speakers. I do, and we bob our heads in rhythm. Jarny raps along with it, of course, while he rolls himself another cigarette. He's always rapping. I couldn't count the number of raps he's written and made me listen to. And it's just as well Constable Rogers didn't decide to give the pickup a random drug search or anything, because we have a case of beer under a cover in the back, which Kalyn bought using his older brother's ID.

We reach the turnoff and head onto the highway. It's a few hundred meters along the road that we take the turn towards the Mish. Kalyn doesn't even brake when he takes the corner. We drift around. He accelerates and the tires scream as we head onto the main street, past the houses lining each side. The dogs of the Mish laze on the road, unmoving for any car.

We pass the empty community center and the toilet block, which sits on its own little field with long grass growing through like heavy pubic hair. Down the hill, we make a turn onto Abby's dirt driveway, following it around the house and through the broken gate into the backyard.

We turn off Biggie Smalls and, no surprise, there's more Biggie Smalls roaring from the house. All the mob is in the backyard. I see Tesha, my girlfriend. She's standing with her best mate, Abby, on the back veranda, drinking the vodka-thing she likes and wearing her white top and black jean shorts, which I like because they highlight her brown thighs.

Jarny carries the case of beer over his shoulder. We head past the fire barrels towards the house. A couple of the boys are piling wood into a heap and offer us a wave.

"Ladies," Kalyn teases as he passes the girls, which is typical of Kalyn. He's always trying to get some. Jarny's more interested in the beer—he's inside already. I place my hand on Tesha's hip and plant a kiss on her cheek.

"Fuck off, you'll ruin my makeup," she says, pressing her elbow to my chest. The jab of pain makes me laugh, and I head inside with Kalyn. Jarny's placed the case on the kitchen bench, and the three of us each rip a beer out of the box like we haven't had anything to drink for days. I notice a few of the girls are helping Abby's sister decorate the Christmas tree. They string fairy lights along the wall and tape them there.

"Jackson, come dance!" Abby calls as she walks through the back door. Abby is the real party girl of the Mish. She's always finding some excuse to get drunk and dance. We weren't really friends before I started going out with Tesha, and now she acts like she's my bestie too—which is pretty annoying, to be honest.

"After a few more," I say, holding up my almost full beer. I throw the cap into the bin by the sink and take a sip.

"Don't be boring," she calls back.

"You know those whitefellas at the pub?" Jarny interrupts.

"Yeah, they were a couple years above me and Kalyn," I say, but I can hardly hear myself talk. I walk back out to the veranda, and Jarny follows me. "The lad with the beard's name is Ethan. He's a bit of a redneck."

The sun bears down on us from the afternoon sky. Every day this summer has entailed a selection of loose clothing and sweat—it must be the hottest summer ever. Through the bushes, we can see the tourists driving past with their trailers and caravans. They're headed farther down the hill to the camping ground by the lake, just like they do every summer.

We head into the backyard and I help Jarny unstack some chairs near the sticks and branches the boys are piling up. The sun goes down past the trees and the shade cools us.

"You thought about next year?" Jarny asks.

"Yeah. Stuff school. Reckon I'll just find a job somewhere."

"Me and Kal will still be there, but."

"Yeah, but you're in Year Ten and Kalyn's smart. I just wanna get a job to make some money, get out of the Mish."

Jarny finishes his beer. "Why? Where you wanna go?"

"I dunno. Somewhere else," I say.

"Cheers to that, then." Jarny taps his empty bottle against mine and I follow him back inside. Tesha's talking with Abby on the couch. They look really deep into it, like they just found out some juicy gossip. I get another beer and spot Kalyn chatting to one of Abby's visiting cousins in the kitchen. He has one hand resting on the bench, with his head tilted just enough to look interested in what she's saying. I know he's trying to pick her up.

I take a sip and turn my attention back to Tesha. Whenever she's gossiping, she always sits forward and uses her hand to express what she's saying—which is exactly what I am seeing right now. Her nails are kept long. Tonight they're glossed with a shiny purple. I should go over there, be a good boyfriend and pretend I'm interested in whatever they're talking about.

Jarny grabs the blasting speaker, carrying it past me and out to the backyard. He doesn't stop despite all the protests from the drunken girls inside.

I'm a little drunk when night comes. Tesha finds me in the backyard and sits on my lap. She smells like the perfume I bought her last month. It's sexy, like a tangy tiger. The backyard is filled with other teenagers from the Mish, and I've been watching Kalyn move from girl to girl, trying his luck.

"He must be horny as hell tonight," I whisper to Tesha. She giggles and starts to kiss me hard, gripping my hair as she does so. I guess Kalyn's not the only horny one tonight.

We leave the backyard and then we're alone in Abby's bedroom. Tesha crawls onto the bed and I crawl on top of her. She pulls my shirt, brings my mouth to hers.

My shirt comes off, then my pants. I unbutton Tesha's shorts and slide them off her legs, drop them to the floor, and kiss her ankles. I take my time and make my way back to her thighs, then to her stomach. She's gripping my hair again. I find her mouth and kiss her. She holds my face against hers. I move my hand from her bare breast to between her legs. She gasps when I touch her. I just keep kissing.

She pulls me onto her body and wraps her legs around my waist. I'm out of breath, but I still kiss her. And it's so hot in this bedroom, my sweat is probably dripping from my skin onto hers.

She kisses me hard again and pulls me against her. She tightens her legs around my waist. I focus. I focus on what I'm doing.

Come on, I think. *Just do it.*

I feel her. I think about feeling her. I think about what she wants me to do, and how much I want to do it. But fuck me, I just can't get hard. I try to breathe slower. Concentrate. I take my hand and try to work it up, as she kisses my forehead and showers me with the warmth of her breath.

"Hurry up," she whispers. And her voice sounds so sexy, I'm almost straining. I look down to her breasts. My hand is getting sore and now I'm just tired. I roll off her and lie beside her on the bed.

"Sorry," I say, almost gasping for air. "I'm too fucking drunk."

"You're always *too fucking drunk*."

I find my breath and can feel the disappointment filling the room. I could laugh at myself. Like, really laugh at myself.

Pathetic.

What sort of a man are you?

"You think I'm ugly or something?" she asks. I can sense a snap in her voice, which pierces me in small stabs.

"No, I'm just drunk." I want to fall into the mattress, let myself go deep into the blackness and never come back. "Do you want to try again, later?"

"No. Forget it."

She stands and puts her clothes back on. I just lie there, naked. I wait for the door to close before I sit up. I know I'm not *too fucking drunk*. I'm tipsy at best. And she isn't ugly. I think she's beautiful. Maybe my body is just broken, or maybe I'm destined to be an abstinent priest or something.

I get dressed and find my way back to the party. Jarny is making out with one of Abby's cousins on the couch, and Kid Cudi is playing now. I watch as Jarny's hand squeezes her hip. It only looks gentle, but I bet it feels nice. I search for Kalyn inside, but I don't see him. I'd half expected it would be him on the couch, with Abby's other cousin.

The lights are dimmed, and the music is way too loud. It must be getting late. I head through the back door and into the backyard, where the music's even louder. Tesha's doing shots with Abby on the grass. She's probably sick of me by now. In all our five months of being together, and two months prior of messing around, I haven't been able to get hard once, not when it's counted. At first I thought I was just nervous. I mean, I was at first. Then I thought it was her—that maybe I just wasn't as attracted to her as I'd thought. But I'm looking at her now as she holds a shot glass filled with vodka, whips it to her mouth, and I know she's beautiful. It isn't her. It's me. I just can't do it.

I leave back through the broken gate and head up the main street of the Mish. Drake is blasting from the speakers now. I can hear him from here. I just hum along to the words as I walk.

I open my front door with caution. It creaks as I close it behind me. I take off my shoes and walk across the wooden floor in my socks, looking to the lounge room as I pass. It's empty as ever, with its couch and chair and television. I savor the image, because I know tomorrow Aunty Pam will be arriving and, just like every Christmas, the house will be filled with little kids—cousins from Sydney.

I walk up the stairs to my bedroom, drop all my clothes to the floor, lie naked on my bed. I toss the blanket away because I won't need it. I feel my penis. It's so useless right now. A letdown. Maybe it just doesn't work at all.

A car horn honks over and over, waking me. It's Christmas Eve, and the morning sun is blinding when I open my eyes. I forgot to pull the fucking curtain across when I went to bed, and now I'm paying for it. Mum's big body booms on the hallway floor, followed by Henry's little rushing feet. As they creak down the stairs, he's asking her if his cousins are here and she's saying yes. I stagger to my clothes, pick them up off the floor, and slide them on.

"Jackson!" I hear Mum call. I start downstairs. Aunty Pam is just inside the doorway, bags in her hands, wearing a purple top and shorts. All the kids run in from behind her, hugging Henry and cheering and yelling as loudly as they can.

"My little sand-eater," Aunty Pam says. I go down to give her a hug and a kiss on the cheek. "How's your art going?"

"I don't really paint so much anymore," I say, looking to my feet.

"Oh. Well, I got a boy who needs to do some art. You can help him out," she says, like I have no say in the matter, like she didn't hear what I just said about not painting so much anymore. "Jackson, this is Tomas. He's living with me for a little while."

She turns to her side to reveal a black boy carrying more bags from her station wagon. He has messy curly hair that looks almost like dreads, like he's never brushed it in his life. His skin is lighter brown than mine, but he has that Koori nose.

"We'll put Henry down here with the boys and you can take Henry's room," Mum says to Aunty Pam. "And we'll put the good mattress in Jackson's room, so Tomas can sleep upstairs away from the kids."

"Who's that?" Henry asks behind me.

"That's Tommy. He just got out of jail," little cousin Bobby whispers, and I feel the strength of my eyebrows as they raise themselves. All the kids barge past Mum and me and race into the house.

Tomas lugs the bags to the doorway and places them on the floor. I extend my hand and Tomas takes it.

9

"Nice to meet ya," I say.

"You too."

I stare at him in his blue polo shirt and sweatpants. He carries a backpack over his shoulders. The hairs on his face look spiky, and the hair on his head sweeps to the sides at his forehead and drapes over his ears.

"Jackson, why don't you take Aunty Pam's and Tomas's stuff upstairs?" Mum asks.

Tomas nods to a duffel bag on the floor next to Aunty Pam's purple traveling bag, and I grab them and head upstairs. He follows, stepping heavily on the wooden stairs. I drop Aunty Pam's bag in Henry's room across the hall and place Tomas's duffel bag against the wall in my room.

"I'll go get you the mattress," I say as he drops his backpack to the floor.

I race back down the staircase and search in the storage space underneath, finding the mattress squeezed into the back corner. I pull it out with all my might. It's thicker than those the kids will sleep on, and I'm annoyed as I drag it back up the stairs. I like having my *own* room. I hate sharing. What if I need to fart or something while I'm in bed? Do I just hold it in forever?

I slide the mattress across my carpet and lay it flat. Tomas drops onto it with a sigh. I fetch him a sheet and blanket and drop them onto the floor beside his mattress, then take one of my two pillows from my bed and hand it to him.

"Make yourself at home," I say.

After a shower, I pass by my bedroom and stop at the doorway. Tomas has kicked off his shoes and rolled onto his side, and he's snoring away. He's not a quiet snorer, either, and it worries me to think he may snore all night. His face has fallen flat and still, and his hair is messing all over my pillow.

I want to wake him, ask him if he really just got out of jail and, if so, what he did to get in there. Maybe we could talk more, about random shit. But I instead stumble down the stairs, ready for the craziness, already able to hear the kids chattering at full volume. An image burns itself into my mind, of Tomas lying there on the mattress.

I think I was thinking something weird when I stared at him.

I think I thought he was cute.

TWO

It takes some adjusting, having all the kids in the house, even though they come every Christmas. They run and laugh and play and swear and just don't stop. They have so much energy.

I help Mum bring in the thin mattresses from the back shed. We carry them into the lounge room and spread them on the floor, between the TV and the couch.

"Jackson," Mum says, "me and Aunty are heading to town to finish off our shopping. Look after the kids—make sure they're all alive when we get back."

She and Aunty Pam practically run out the front door and I'm left in charge of all the kids. All eight of them! I just sit them in the lounge room and put on *The Incredibles*. They pile onto their mattresses and the couch, reciting all the words. It's so annoying. My head feels like there's a blunt pair of scissors twisting at my temples.

I bake them some chicken nuggets and side it with tomato sauce. Sleeping Beauty (Tomas) joins us on the couch just as the boys swarm on the nuggets. I only eat one in the end. One chicken nugget. One.

Tomas is quiet as he gets comfortable on the couch, at the other end of the assembly of boys with their butts planted. All of them turn their heads together when Mum and Aunty Pam come through the front door.

"Cover your eyes," Mum says as they pass. I watch as the kids all *do* cover their eyes.

After a headache of a day dodging the energy of the kids, I'm happy when night comes. The comfort of my bed is hollow, though, because Tomas is snoring on my floor. And it's so hot in here that I don't know how the hell he managed to fall asleep in the first place.

Behind Henry's bedroom door, Aunty Pam is snoring too, but she's not as loud as the whipper-snipper on my floor.

I stumble down the stairs with a dry throat. Henry and our cousins are sleeping on their mattresses. I gaze over at Henry as he sleeps, sharing a blanket with little Bobby. I remember being his age. I remember being so excited for summer because it meant all the cousins were coming to stay. We would run around and spray ourselves with the hose, walk our wet and sandy feet through the house, and get shouted at by the Aunts and Uncles and Mum—even by my father, before Mum got rid of him. I remember not wanting to sleep in my own bed, because I preferred to sleep downstairs with Kalyn and our other cousins. We would watch cartoons all night on the TV until one of the Aunties stormed in and told us to turn it off.

I take a sip from the tap in the kitchen, then creep back up the stairs, stepping as lightly as I can. The stairs creak anyway, because the wood is old and I'm not the smallest of boys. I reach the top and Mum's door swings open. She's carrying a big box wrapped in Christmas paper and gasps as she spots me.

"Jesus, Jackson, you scared the shit outta me. Come give me a hand with this, will ya?"

I take one end of the box and we carry it down the stairs together.

"Gotta get these under the tree before I pass out," she says. "I forgot how much Pam can drink."

The box is heavy, and the stairs creak loudly under our combined weight. We sneak past the lounge and kitchen to the living room, which is lit by the colorful Christmas lights decorating our tree. We place the box underneath and then make a few more trips back and forth, until the presents fill the floor beneath the tree. And there are so many presents. I'm jealous of these spoiled kids.

"Good night," Mum says once we're done and back upstairs. As she closes her door, I get a peek inside her room at all the artwork she's made. Years' worth of canvases—dot paintings—rest piled against the wall, while some hang above from nails. When I think of Mum, I always think of her as an artist.

I go to my wardrobe and get out the two small wrapped presents stashed there, labeled *Mum* and *Henry*. I tiptoe back downstairs and place them on one of the branches of the tree.

The kids scream down the house, because it's Christmas morning, and Christmas is the most exciting morning in any kid's year. They belt out their joy from downstairs as they rip open their presents.

Tomas's mattress is already empty. I take my shirt and shorts from the floor, then check my phone. No messages from Tesha.

No messages from anyone. I head downstairs and pour myself a glass of water, dodging the kids zooming around the house with their new Nerf guns and lightsabers.

"There you are, Jackson," Aunty Pam says. "Give Aunty a kiss." I give her a kiss on the cheek and a smile. "How's school going? You must be nearly finished now, right?"

"Just finished Year Eleven. Not sure about going back next year," I say.

"Well," Mum interrupts as she enters the kitchen, "you wanna get a job quick, boy, or you're going straight back there." She checks the oven, and the aroma of cooking meat fills the house. I'm starving right away. I notice Mum's wearing the necklace I got her for Christmas.

"Santa treated you all right," I say. She smiles and presses her fingers over the locket. I've placed a photo of me and Henry inside.

"If you see Santa, tell him I'm very thankful," she says, planting a kiss on my cheek.

The time comes for Christmas lunch, and we bring another table from Mum's room into the kitchen. Juvie-boy Tomas sits opposite me, beside little cousin Bobby and his ten-months-older brother, Ryan, who has his new Darth Vader mask resting on the top of his head.

"Before we start," Mum tells us, "let's say a prayer."

All the kids close their eyes and force their palms into the praying position. Tomas's eyes dart to mine. His face has whitened and I start to think maybe he's never heard someone say a prayer before, or prayed himself. I mean, I'm not all that keen on religion or whatever, but I've prayed and meant it before, and

I think it's kind of a nice thing to do, even if you don't fully believe in God. And besides, Mum takes *thanking the Lord* very seriously. I close my eyes, hoping Tomas will do the same, for his sake.

"Dear God," Mum says, "we give our thanks for the food we are about to eat. We thank you for a good, safe year, and for all the great things you've given our family. Please watch over us in the year to come . . . and tell Jackson he should go back to school and not throw his future away."

I nearly choke on my own spit as the laughter bursts its way out.

"Amen," Mum says.

"Amen," everyone repeats.

All the kids dig into their food and I'm ravenous. Tomas is ravenous too. He's a loud chewer, and he chews with his mouth open, which I'm sure would piss off Mum if only she was noticing. She's always going on about table manners. I kind of feel like throwing my fork at him. Not the pointed end first, obviously.

"So, Tomas, what's it like living in Sydney?" Mum asks.

Tomas looks up from his plate. "It's all right," he answers.

"Are you still going to school?"

"Yeah, most of the time."

"What do you do when you're not at school?"

"I dunno," Tomas says. "Hang out with my mates, kick back in my room."

"He does nothing *good* when he's not at school," Aunty Pam interrupts. "Which is why he'll be going more from now on. Right, Tomas?"

Tomas nods and we share a look of lecture fatigue.

After my stomach settles, I help Aunty Pam hang out the

washing in the backyard. It's a shitty, boring, sweaty job—one I think would be better suited to juvie-boy. But it's not the worst thing in the world, because Aunty Pam is making me laugh. After a few of her stories, though—including the one about how she and Mum spilled Nan's ashes on a taxi driver while they were drunk—she gives me the look that tells me I'm in for another lecture. At least me and Tomas have one thing in common—we both get lectured by old black women.

"Back when we were kids, we didn't have the same chances as you kids these days. I never really knew a blackfella who finished school until I met your Uncle. But you kids these days got a chance. Everything's different now."

"I know," I say, rolling my eyes.

Mum comes out and sets up a big canvas on the grass, then she lays out her paints, all spat onto a plastic sheet, with her brushes of all different sizes stacked in a little bucket of water. This is the artwork she and Aunty Pam work on every time Aunty Pam comes to visit. It's of a river, with three mothers on one side and their children on the other. It's something about the Stolen Generations, the Aboriginal kids who were taken from their families by the government. Mum explained it to me when they first started it, but I can't really remember the details of what she said—they've been working on it for years. I'm starting to doubt they'll ever finish the thing.

"Jackson," Mum says, "why don't you get Kalyn and take all the boys down the river for a couple hours?"

"The river? But I'm stuffed from lunch. We're all stuffed."

"Just take 'em down there, so they can try those new inflatables and snorkels out."

"I'm tired, though," I say, throwing my head back as Aunty Pam follows me inside.

"Just do what your mother tells ya," Aunty Pam tells me. "Give me and your mum a break so we can do some painting, yeah?"

"Fine," I say. And then I announce loudly to the whole house, "Boys, we are going for a swim!"

Their cheers ring out from every direction.

"You going with them, Tommy?" Aunty Pam asks. She's still following me.

"Nah, I should get started on this project while I got some quiet," Tomas says.

While I got some quiet. He sounds like an old man.

I text Kalyn to drive us, and before long his truck pulls up out front. He greets all the kids with high-fives as they pile into the back. We speed off, out of the Mish and onto the highway. Henry and Bobby try out their goggles in the back seat. We turn into town and pass the footy fields, then take a left at the traffic lights before the shops and head along the dirt road through the bush.

I'm worried that there'll be townspeople and tourists there, but when we pull into the car park there are no other cars. The boys don't mess around—they run straight from the truck to the river and dive into the current. Kalyn and I walk to the water and there's still no one about, not a soul. We have it all to ourselves.

"Get anything for Christmas, cuz?" Kalyn asks.

"Mum just gave me a hundred bucks last payday," I say. I don't mind, though. A hundred bucks is never a bad present.

"Far out. Me too."

The current is strong as I walk into the river and lower myself onto my knees. Tiny rocks glisten on the riverbed. I reach down and scoop up a handful, hold my hand to the surface and let the rocks flow away with the water. The water is shallow, but that's fine considering it's usually all dried up in summer.

I dunk my head under and join Kalyn back on the bank. We sit with our feet in the water. Henry, Bobby, and a few of the other boys venture into the bush.

"Don't go too far!" I shout as they disappear.

"Me and Jarny are gonna head down to the camping ground tonight. You in?" Kalyn asks.

"Yeah. Anything to get away from these kids."

Kalyn chuckles. My thoughts turn to Tesha as I lie back on the sand. I should text her, right? I should be a good boyfriend and get myself hard enough to have sex with her, just like she wants. I wish it was as easy as *wishing* then *getting*, but I worry I will never be able to get hard with anyone. Maybe I should go to a doctor and get some Viagra.

The trees' branches and leaves sway against each other in the breeze. It's such a calming sound. Then screams ring out from the bush, and I know it's the kids. Kalyn jumps to his feet.

"Jackson!" I hear from somewhere among the trees, and I'm up and gone, into the bush.

THREE

I follow the cries of my name and spot the boys ahead on the path. Three of them are trying to carry Bobby. His little arms and legs flail about.

"Help, Jackson!" Henry screams.

Bobby's face is red and there are tears all over his cheeks. I reach him and halt my feet like I've just used a handbrake.

"What? What's wrong?"

"Snake," Bobby's brother Ryan says, with such urgency and panic. "Snake got him. Red-belly, I saw it!"

I take Bobby into my arms and cradle him. There's a small gathering of blood behind his ankle. I don't know what to do. I put him down, rip off my shirt, and wrap it tight around his leg.

"Kalyn!" I shout, but he's right behind me. "Get the car started. We gotta go."

I pick up Bobby again. He feels heavier. He's still crying. The other kids race past, ahead of me. I move as quickly as I can along the path, ignoring the rocks and twigs pressing into my bare feet.

I reach the riverside and hear the truck kick over. Kalyn is in the driver's seat and the kids pile in.

"Quickly!" someone yells. "Before he dies!"

I slide Bobby onto the laps of the boys sitting on the back seat and jump into the front. Kalyn takes off and we speed along the dirt road. My hands are shaking and my heart is beating so fast and hard it could break my chest.

We drive out of the bush and the dirt road turns to pavement. We speed along, hit a red light as we come into town. I turn back to Bobby. He's asleep. Well, he looks like he's sleeping.

"Bobby?" I ask. He just moans. "It's all right—we ain't too far."

The light turns green and Kalyn spins the wheels.

"Careful," I say. I look out the back window to see the boys in the back, holding on for their lives. "Slow down."

Everyone on the main street—locals as well as the tourists, carrying their shopping bags, pushing their trolleys—looks at us as we pass them: a truck carrying a bunch of Aboriginal kids in the back, speeding through town.

We turn another corner. It feels like we're going to roll, but Kalyn straightens up. The medical center is just ahead. I turn back to Bobby. He's still moaning.

Kalyn slams on his brakes. I'm out of the passenger door before we've even come to a complete stop. I wrench open the back door and drag Bobby out, take him in my arms. He starts crying again as the other kids jump out and race ahead into the center, their shouts echoing from inside.

Kalyn beats me to the door and holds it open. The air-conditioning hits me as I rush inside. The receptionist is trying to quiet the boys, but she stops and comes out from behind her desk when she sees me.

"He got bit by a red-belly," I say.

A nurse wheels a hospital bed out to us, and I lay Bobby down. He's still crying.

"His name's Bobby," I tell the nurse.

"Bobby, I need you to calm down," she says.

Another nurse joins her and examines the wound. "Red-belly black snake?" he asks.

I nod.

"It's okay. He should be fine."

They wheel him away through some doors and I follow. We go into a room and a doctor arrives. It's all a blur, what happens next. I can hardly concentrate on staying still in this room.

"Is he your brother?" the first nurse asks.

"Cousin," I say. "He and his family are visiting for Christmas."

"You should go give his mum or dad a call. He'll be okay."

I'm still hot and I feel like I'm bouncing, even though I'm sitting quite still, on the edge of the seat. I walk back to reception, where Kalyn is sitting with all seven of the other boys.

"I called Aunty Kris. She and Aunty Pam are on the way," Kalyn says as I take a seat beside him.

"Aunty Pam's gonna kill me."

Jude, one of Bobby's older brothers, asks, "Is Bobby gonna die?"

"No," I say. "But *I* might."

He just sits there with his eyes drooping and his mouth sagging.

I take his hand. "Come on, he'll want you to be there."

Little Ryan springs to his feet too, and with Jude's hand still in mine, I take them both back through the corridor to the emergency room. The first nurse from earlier is feeling Bobby's forehead with the back of her hand.

"His mum's on the way," I say to her. She spots Jude and Ryan, both shielding half their bodies behind my legs. "These are Bobby's big brothers, Jude and Ryan. They wanted to come check on him."

The nurse beckons Jude and Ryan to Bobby's bedside and helps them up so they can sit beside him. They both look like they're about to cry as they stare at Bobby, and I feel my heart breaking. I almost wish Aunty Pam *would* kill me, so I won't have to live with this feeling. I sit down on the chair and watch over them. Bobby's chest is rising and falling but it's slow.

"He's just sleeping. He'll feel a little sick from the bite, but he'll be okay," the nurse tells Jude and Ryan. They stay quiet. The nurse leaves us, telling me to call her if we need anything.

How about a plane ticket to Fiji or something? Away from where I wait in failure.

I go back to the waiting room. I've barely got my ass on the seat when Mum and Aunty Pam burst through the doors. They glance at us but go straight to reception. They've both got paint on their arms. The first nurse comes out and takes Aunty Pam off to the emergency room. Mum comes to sit beside me and Kalyn.

"You all right?" she asks.

I just nod. I feel the tension releasing now that she's here.

"Good Christmas present for your Aunty," she teases, nudging me with her elbow.

I try not to smile, but one finds its way to my face.

Mum heads into the corridor leading to the emergency room just as two people walk out of it. It's Jasper, the tall, lanky gay kid from school. He's with his mum, I think.

Jasper was Jarny's biology partner last year, so we'd always tease Jarny about spending so much time with the gay kid and ask him when he was having his coming-out party. Jarny hated it.

Even in the medical center, Jasper has his fingernails painted black, and I think he's wearing some eyeliner.

"Hey, boys," he says as he passes by.

"Bit sick?" Kalyn asks.

"Just a bit of food poisoning."

He offers us a smile, but my body takes over and forces me to avoid making eye contact with him.

"Food poisoning?" Kalyn whispers to me as Jasper and his mum leave the center. "Probably got his shampoo bottle stuck in his ass."

I force a chuckle. "Maybe," I say.

Mum comes back from the emergency room. "Kalyn, why don't you give us a lift home? Pam's gonna stay with Bobby and his brothers, but he'll be fine."

The rest of us pile into the truck again and head back to the Mish. I feel exhausted, like the snake injected its venom into me too. We pull up out front of my house just as the sun sets.

"Still wanna come to the camping ground?" Kalyn asks.

"Why don't you stay at Kal's place tonight, give yourself a break from the kids?" Mum interrupts.

I nod, and she and the kids get out of the truck. Henry waves as we drive away. I wonder how I would have reacted if it had been Henry who was bitten, and the thought scares me. I stay in the thought until we get to Kalyn's house down the road, when I realize I left my shirt at the medical center with Bobby.

Kalyn offers me one of his shirts, as well as a beer. I down a quarter of it in one go. Never before have I wanted a beer so badly.

We sit at the table and chairs in the backyard. Kalyn's parents and little sisters are inside watching *Shrek*. We can hear it from the backyard.

"I texted Jarny," Kalyn says. "He's gonna come round after dinner."

I realize my phone's in my pocket and I haven't looked at my messages since we went to the river. I pull it out and there are four from Tesha.

What you up to?

Ur mum said your at the river, when you getting back?

Come over.

We need to talk . . .

I get stuck feeling annoyed at her use of *your* instead of *you're* in her second message. But then I reread them and a worry grows in my stomach. I turn off my phone and finish my beer.

Kalyn and I play Xbox in the lounge room after his family goes to bed, keeping the volume down. Jarny taps at the window and scares the shit out of us. He lets himself in through the front door and sits with us on the couch.

"I was down there earlier," Jarny says, "at the camping ground. There are a few new kids, and Troy and Jasmine are back again. Troy said he's having a few drinks tonight and is inviting the other kids. I said we'd come."

"I dunno," I say. "I don't really feel like talking to white people right now."

"We can just wait till they go to sleep and go raid their coolers?" Kalyn suggests.

"Yeah, okay," I say.

"Fine, then," Jarny says, disappointed. "I'll text Troy to let him know we ain't coming."

Good old Troy. He's always thought he's very cool. We all hang out when his family comes to camp here—but he always comes at you with that low-class bogan accent. And he uses the word *mate* way too much. I remember last year he said he wanted to be a cop, and it didn't surprise me at all. I could picture him in a blue uniform, pulling me over for no reason one night, then putting me against the side of the car for a good old strip search.

Midnight comes and we turn off the Xbox. We leave our shoes at the house and walk barefoot. Jarny lights himself a rolled cigarette as we hit the road.

"What you reckon about Jasmine? Think she'd like a *walk on the dark side*?" Jarny asks, his voice cutting through the quiet of the Mish.

"She don't date blackfellas," I tease.

"Who said anything about dating?"

"You're too short and your nose is too big," Kalyn says. "She'd want a tall, dark, handsome lad . . . like me."

Jarny gives Kalyn a gentle punch on the shoulder and they push each other round a bit. I continue on down the hill, into the darkness.

Through the bushes, I can see the campfires. I start down a pathway through the bush. It's so hard to see, but we've walked this path a thousand times. We weave around the trees and over the dried leaves and twigs, stopping in the bush a few meters from the campsite's edge. All the campervans are dark. The pitched tents are spread through the clearing. Someone is playing music quietly, but there's no one out. Everyone is asleep and all the fires are dying.

I spot Troy's camp. His father always likes to put up solar-powered fairy lights, which he hangs as a fence round their camp. There's their cooler, under a table beside the campervan. I know his parents are asleep in there, and that Troy's in the tent a few meters from it. I step out first but direct Jarny to the cooler, because he's the skinniest and sneaks the lightest. He opens the lid and pulls out two beers.

We move on to another campsite, where we almost walk over the top of a cooler just sitting there in the open, like it's begging to be robbed. It's filled with vodka cruisers, so I take one of those. We follow the pathway to the lake, picking up speed and disappearing into the bush.

At the lake we have to breathe our laughter away. I love the adrenaline rush—it makes me feel so alive. I could laugh and scream and run as fast as my legs can handle. And it soothes the heavy feeling of regret about Bobby getting bitten today.

We walk along the edge of the lake and sit behind a rock. The lake is so wide and dark, and the moonlight skims across its surface. Jarny hands one of his beers to Kalyn, and I drink the vodka cruiser. We just sit there. The sky has opened right up. There are no clouds at all, only the stars clustering across the black sky.

"I heard on TV that some of the stars are dead," Kalyn says.

"What?" me and Jarny ask at the same time.

"Yeah, like when they get old and explode . . . it was something about the light taking so long to get to Earth, or some shit like that."

"So, if some stars are dead, that means some are alive, right?" Jarny asks. "Like, *living things?*"

"Hmm. Nah, that sounds stupid. Forget it," Kalyn says.

We finish our drinks and follow the lake around to where it connects with the beach, then head along the sand towards the rocks at the end. It would be a much longer walk if we weren't tipsy, but it's nice, just feeling the warmth still trapped in the sand beneath my bare feet as I sink into it with every step.

At the rocks, we find the wooden staircase in the darkness. I climb first, up to the cliff top. Jarny and Kalyn follow, and we stare for a moment at the sea, rolling in its waves of black, cut by the white foam when it's caught in the moonlight. I could fall down there, feel the wind through my whole body, hit the water with a bang, and swim all the way down.

We head along the pathway through the bush. It's dark but we know the way, following the path past the rusty tap. We reach the end of the bush and come to the Mish, just above where the road turns downhill towards the camping ground, right next to the bush path that leads right up to the top of the mountain.

"You stayin' the night?" Kalyn asks as Jarny leaves us for his house.

"Nah. I'll just go home."

"I'll see ya in the morning for the races," he says. "Make sure you dress all right."

"Always do," I say.

I watch as he disappears inside his house, then continue up the main street of the Mish. Home's only a few houses away, but I dawdle. For some reason, I keep thinking of what Kalyn said about Jasper when he left the medical center—about getting a shampoo bottle stuck in his ass. It's not the worst thing I've heard him say, and hell, I've said worse myself, but I guess I'm feeling a little bothered by it. Maybe I'm just a bit sensitive right now because of the snake incident. Maybe.

I arrive home. The kids are all asleep, and there's Bobby next to Henry. I wonder if he hates me.

I head up the staircase and it creaks louder than ever. I'm a bit wobbly, but I make it to my room. Tomas is snoring, so I sneak past his mattress and fall onto my bed. He's sweaty tonight. It's not *horrible* body odor, but I am definitely smelling sweat. I'm drowsy, but I see him clearly in the moonlight coming through my window.

As annoyed as I am at him being here, I kind of feel sorry for him. He must have had a family of his own once, and now he's a million miles away from anywhere, with a bunch of strangers, sharing a room with someone and sleeping on a floor. I wonder if he's dangerous, if he has dark thoughts. I wonder what he did to end up in juvie.

FOUR

Boxing Day is cooler. All the kids have woken me up again, and Tomas is not on his mattress. His blanket is just rolled to the side like a discarded piece of meat; he could have at least made an effort and folded it or something. Or how about a *thank you for letting me take up all your space?*

Downstairs, the kids fill the lounge room, planted in front of the television, eating cereal and spilling milk all over their chins. I sit with them and eat some Coco Pops. Mum informs me that Tomas has gone for a walk, though I don't care to know.

I hit the shower. My feet are dirty as hell. I watch the dirt wash away, wrap myself in my towel, and lay my nice white buttoned shirt and black pants out on my bed. I rustle through my old worn shoes to find the nice black ones and plug my phone into its charger. The screen lights up with another message from Tesha.

Jackson. We need to talk.

I ignore it and get dressed. The shirt feels tighter on my stomach. It must have been the Christmas luncheon—or perhaps it's the alcohol I've been consuming since I decided I'll be quitting school.

I drop my phone and wallet into my pockets and head back downstairs. A Nerf-gun bullet whacks me in the neck and stings like hell. Henry's in the kitchen doorway and I lunge for him, but he's too fast.

Bobby's at the kitchen table with Aunty Pam. He's coloring in some picture of a cow, but he's coloring the body black and the spots yellow and red to match the colors in the Aboriginal flag.

"He's a future activist," I tease. "How you doin', Bobby? You all right?"

"Yeah," he says. I remember that I'm actually terrible at making conversation with kids. I never figured out how to talk to them and make it sound like I care, even though I usually do care. *Usually.*

"Why don't you go find Tomas?" Aunty Pam says. "He went to the beach, I think. Go keep him company."

"I can't—sorry, Aunt. I've gotta run."

I can't get out the front door quick enough. I head for Kalyn's house, but he and Jarny are already walking my way. They're dressed up too. Kalyn is wearing his blue button-up shirt and blue jeans, sunglasses tucked into his collar. Jarny's wearing a white shirt and yellow pants, with his hair gelled. He's smoking a rolled cigarette.

"Lookin' good, boys," I say. Jarny offers me a cigarette, but I decline. "Let's go the back way, yeah?"

We turn around and head down the hill.

"Owen said they'll meet us there," Kalyn says.

"Owen's back?" I ask.

"Yeah, he got out on Christmas Eve," Kalyn says.

"You know if Tesha's coming?"

"She's your woman—you should know." Jarny laughs.

I pull out my phone and open her last message. I stare at it for a moment, then text a reply.

I'll come over after the races.

She replies right away.

Good.

I have an uneasy feeling in my stomach. More than just uneasy. I could throw up if it was any stronger. I focus on my steps as we start along the dirt track that leads around the mountain and through the bush.

"Bet ya I'll get a kiss from a white girl today," Kalyn says as he flicks on his sunglasses.

Jarny bursts into laughter. "A kiss? I'll be in the bathroom having an orgy before you get a kiss from a white girl," he says.

"Who would you bet on, Jackson?" Kalyn asks.

"You're both fucking idiots."

We pass the camping ground, come to the bottom of the mountain, then follow the dirt track past the farms and paddocks. The smell of cow shit is strong in the air. Clouds shield us from the sun and threaten a rainstorm, but a trail of sweat still grows along my spine. We cross the wooden bridge over the river, follow the bank till we reach the car park we were at on Christmas Day, and follow the road from there into town. Maybe an hour has passed, but Jarny's terrible jokes and Kalyn's unprecedented confidence have helped the time breeze by.

The town is packed with tourists, talking so loudly that I could probably hear every one of their conversations if I stopped and listened. They line the main street all the way from the footy fields down to the beach at the end of the road. I dread even seeing the beach, all of them swimming and sunbathing so closely together.

We pass the pub, head away from the main street, and see the line for the races. Rodney and Perry, two men from the Mish, are the security guards. They let us pass with a nod and a handshake.

We jostle through the crowd. People are lining up for drinks at the various outdoor bars, and to play the gambling machines that stand in the spaces between the bars. Everyone is dressed up, and the air is a mixture of deodorant, perfume, sweat, and alcohol. Everyone I see is white. Some of them are tourists, but most of them are locals. I recognize a few people from school who graduated this year.

I spot my cousin Owen, who's just had a short stint in prison. I haven't seen him in a few months. He's put on more weight, I think. He's sitting with the mob from the Mish on a grassy hill. Abby and her girls sit on the plastic chairs, but Tesha's not there. Me, Jarny, and Kalyn join them, sitting on the grass.

"How's it goin', brother?" Owen asks as I shake his hand. I bounce against his big belly when he pulls me in for a hug. He's drunk already. "You right, cuz?"

I just nod.

"Good to see ya again."

Kalyn takes my and Jarny's money and heads back into the crowd with his brother's ID in hand. Jarny rolls a cigarette, and we watch the people on the racecourse leading their horses around the track. A warm-up, I guess.

Kalyn returns with our cups of beer held in a plastic tray, Troy following behind him. Just as I expected, Troy's arms have grown in muscle since I saw him last year. His face looks bigger, somehow. His head is shaved, and I can't help but notice the blisters on his palm when he shakes my hand.

"Who are these faggots?" he asks, his eyes narrowed and his head cocked to the side. There's that bogan voice of his. Like always, it sounds like he's forcing the accent, exaggerating it, on purpose.

"No faggots here," Jarny says, jumping into his boxing stance. Troy does the same, and I really hope no one is watching as they play-wrestle on the grass for one second too long.

"How's it goin', boys?" Troy asks me and Jarny once they're done.

"All right," we say at the same time.

"Yeah, I'm just here with me old man. How come youse haven't come seen us yet?"

"We were gonna yesterday but, you know, had Christmas stuff on," Jarny says.

"Youse should come tonight. I'm getting some of the other campers round for a drink. Lots of newbies this year. They'd love youse."

"Yeah, we'll head down later," I say, mostly just to get rid of him and his bogan voice.

"Sweet, mate. Just follow the music." He disappears into the crowd.

A gunshot sounds, and the horses begin to race around the track. Kalyn edges forward, his betting slip in his hand. Everyone in the crowd howls and shouts, their cries echoing into the sky.

Most people have jumped up, their own betting slips in their hands. The drama is thick in the air. It's exhilarating.

The horses race around the bend directly in front of us, jockeys firmly planted on their backs. There are at least ten horses racing, all a blur. Their hooves beat down on the dirt, their breaths heavy as they puff and struggle for air. They race towards the finish line to a chorus of people cheering and swearing like animals. They pass the line and the winner is called over the speaker.

"Goddammit. Fourth," Kalyn shouts beside me.

I just sip my beer while Jarny cracks up. He's rolled back and holds his stomach. I start laughing too and spit out some of my beer.

"Stop it, assholes," Kalyn says. He leaves to put on another bet while we collect ourselves.

"Did you talk to Tesha?" Abby asks me. Her lipstick is bright red, her makeup is heavy, and she's almost frowning as she looks at me.

"Nah," I say. "Not yet."

"You should. She wants to talk to you."

"I know."

I can't enjoy myself after that. Later I catch the bus back to the Mish with Jarny and Kalyn, after a quick stop at the bottle shop. I'm tipsy now, and I feel like crying, because I know when I get off the bus, I'll have to go to Tesha's house.

The bus slowly empties until there are only a few other people left. We take the turn to the Mish as the sun sets in the distance, passing Tesha's house a few doors down from the sign announcing entrance to the Mish. The bus stops at the community center, where some young boys and girls throw their basketball at the hoops erected in the car park, and Kalyn, Jarny, and I get off.

Kalyn turns to me with his case of beer. "Wanna head down to the camping ground with us? Or you gonna go change first?"

"I've gotta go to Tesha's. I'll come down later."

I turn and walk away. I think they know what's happening. Maybe Kalyn saw it in my eyes. He knows me well enough to be able to tell when I'm scared. Hell, he's known me for as long as I've collected memories. And Jarny's been with us at the Mish since he was ten. He only started at our school two years ago, but we've gotten to be good mates since then. Surely they sensed the worry deep inside me, now growing with each step I take closer to Tesha's house.

Her front door is open, with the screen door still shut. The TV's loud enough inside to hear from the front gate. I take a deep breath and knock on the screen door. Tesha's sitting on the couch with her little brother and mum.

"Hey," she says, arriving at the door.

"Hey."

"Let's go to my room."

I give a wave to Tesha's mum and brother and follow her up the hallway, which is lit only by the light shining from her half-open bedroom door. The darkness envelops me.

FIVE

I follow Tesha into her room and she closes the door. I sit on her bed and she sits beside me. Her hand falls onto my knee and I rub my eyes. My knuckles feel dirty as I press them against my eyelids. But I don't care.

"Jackson." I keep my eyes closed but take away my knuckles. "I'm sorry. It's just not working for me anymore," she says.

I feel the tears coming already. I hold my eyes shut tight.

"I love you, but . . ." Every word she speaks is a knife digging into my chest. ". . . I don't feel the same way I used to."

She gently squeezes my knee, and I open my eyes. My tears have subsided for now, but it feels like I've been holding my breath for hours.

"Are you okay?" she asks. Her voice is so soft. My sadness is still there, but now I feel comfort too. I just nod to her.

"I get it," I say. "It's all good."

She hugs me, and I let my head rest on her shoulder. I could just stay there forever, because I know that when she lets go we're done. I don't want to be done. I don't want to be alone again, but I don't think I can give her what she wants.

When she pulls away, she wipes away her tears. I'm puzzled for a moment, then I understand: She cares. I can see it. I can feel it.

"Guess it just wasn't meant to be," I say and smile.

She smiles back. "Not right now, anyway."

I stand and sniffle the tears away before they can escape. My mouth is dry and my face feels hot. My nose is runny, so I let my sleeves down and wipe it all away.

"You sure you're okay?" she asks.

"Yeah. All good."

I leave her house and stop for a moment on the road. A raindrop falls on my forehead. It starts to sprinkle down. The clouds look almost purple as nighttime falls, and the lone streetlight of the Mish ignites near the community center. I need a drink.

Passing my house, I can hear the kids inside, shouting and playing without a care in the world. I just keep walking. My feet are so sore, so I kick off my shoes. I leave them in the gutter as I pass some of the dogs that laze on the side of the road.

I know Kalyn and Jarny have already gone to the camping ground. I keep walking, pull off my socks, and leave them on the road too. I have more at home. I loosen the buttons of my shirt and let the breeze flow through me. The tears threaten to come again, but I breathe them down.

I walk down the hill. The bush looks so dark and endless, like it could swallow me into its belly and I would never be seen again. Maybe I want that. Maybe that would make me feel all right again, to just be gone forever so I can't disappoint anyone anymore.

I find the pathway and start along the dirt. The fires and

lights of the campsites bleed through the black trees, and music is playing from Troy's. I walk towards the fairy lights, following the music.

Jarny's laughing. He's loud and wheezy as always, but it actually feels good to hear his laughter. He's probably laughing at his own joke, to be honest.

I arrive at Troy's camp and see Jarny talking to a white girl. They've set up a circle of camping chairs, which surrounds the fire in the fire pit. Troy spots me as he drops a handful of sticks onto the flames.

"Jacko, mate, glad you could make it!"

Jacko. No one has ever called me that. Ever.

I plant my ass on a chair next to Kalyn. He takes a beer from the case at his feet and hands it to me. I pour most of it down my throat in one go.

"You all right?" he asks.

"Yeah. All good."

Jasmine comes over. She looks as if she's aged ten years since last Christmas, even though she's about a year younger than me. She's wearing makeup, and I think she has fake eyelashes on.

"Hey," she says.

I stand to hug her. "Hey. Long time, no see."

"I reckon! I've missed you boys."

"Have you, now?"

She goes back to her seat and I scan the rest of the chairs. The twins, Matt and Andy, are here. They're identical, and I used to have the hardest time telling them apart, till Matt grew somewhat taller and got a much shorter haircut. They offer me a wave, and I down the rest of my beer. It tastes like shit, but I drink it anyway.

"Grab us another one," I say, holding out my hand. Kalyn passes me another bottle. I open it and take a swig, but then decide to pace myself. I'm feeling a bit clearer now.

I see there are two new girls. They sit together, and while one of them was talking to Jarny when I arrived, they are now whispering to each other. They must be sisters, because they both have brown wavy hair and pointy noses. They're both drinking vodka cans and they look older than us, probably Troy's age.

My thoughts turn to Tesha and my *failures* with her. Maybe I was just burdened by the feeling of being in a relationship, the pressure of needing to give part of myself to someone else. Maybe I could go over there, chat to one of the girls, get her to like me. I wonder if either of them would want to sleep with an Aboriginal boy.

I take another sip of beer and dwell on the thought. They're very attractive girls. Their parents probably work office jobs and earn a lot of money. Maybe they've never really interacted with Aboriginal boys before. Maybe it would excite them.

I realize there's a boy sitting beside them—one I don't recognize. He looks kind of awkward, not talking to anyone, just listening in on the conversations happening around him. His hair is unbrushed and dangles over his ears. He holds a beer in his hand but doesn't seem to be sipping it.

"Oi, white boy," I say.

He turns to me, looking into my eyes. I'm an idiot because I don't have any planned follow-up for my *oi, white boy*. He gives me a small wave.

"Come sit over here," I say. He takes a seat in the empty chair beside me and I offer him a handshake. "I'm Jackson."

"Levi," he says. There's a slight smile at the corner of his mouth.

"How old are you?"

"Ninety-two," he says, and it's the funniest thing I've ever heard. "Nah, I'm sixteen. *Sweet sixteen.*"

"Cool," I say, and I realize I'm a bit nervous. "I'm seventeen."

"Cool," he says. He takes a sip of his beer and I sip mine too.

"Where are you from?" I ask.

"Sydney. Well, Manly, actually."

"How's that?"

"It's fine. It's good to get away, though."

"Yeah, it would be. I was thinking of moving to Sydney one day."

"Why? It's so nice here."

"Yeah. It's home. But I need to get out, I think. I dunno. My Aunty and little cousins are visiting from Sydney. We stayed at their place once when I was little, and I think I liked it."

The fire crackles loudly in a pause between songs on Troy's speakers.

"I never seen you here before," I say.

"It's our first time. We usually go a bit farther south, but we found this place by accident. I was talking to Matt and Andy, and they said they found it by accident as well. So, I have a theory," he says, leaning in.

"What's your theory?"

"Well, Matt and Andy's dad is a bank manager, and my dad's a bank manager, so I think this place has some sort of magical way of luring in bank managers."

"That's silly." I laugh, then take another sip from my beer.

"Yeah, but a *silly* coincidence! Maybe I'm just drunk."

I laugh again. He's funny. "Aren't white parents usually pretty strict about drinking and stuff?"

"Are black parents not?"

"Well, yeah, but I guess I'm a bit of a rebel."

"I'm a rebel too," he says, slouching back in his chair like a seventies gangster.

"You don't look like a rebel."

"Okay. Maybe I'm a lower class of rebel." He laughs.

I finish my beer and take another. Jarny starts dancing when Biggie Smalls comes over the speakers. He raps along with Biggie and doesn't miss a beat. Troy is egging him on, and I worry about the noise—that Levi's parents will come over and drag him back to where everything is safe and innocent.

"Everything all right with Tesha?" Kalyn asks, and his voice seems to come out of nowhere. It surprises me to realize I forgot about Tesha. I forgot to think about how sad I was.

"Um, it's not the best."

Kalyn nods, and we all just keep drinking until Kalyn is up dancing on the dirt with Troy and Jasmine and Jarny and one of the new girls. Matt and Andy are sharing a joke with the other new girl.

"Levi, come dance!" Jasmine calls.

The girls drag Levi to the improvised dance floor. He sort of sways his arms and hips for a moment, then he stumbles past me to the bushes for a piss. He yelps and I turn around to see he's fallen over backwards. I go and help him, taking hold of his shoulders, lifting him to his feet.

"You right?"

"Something moved in the bushes," he says, rebuttoning his shorts. He's pissed all over himself.

"You might wanna go change pants," I say.

He looks down and sighs. "Far out," he says. He staggers away, disappearing into the dark, presumably off to his campsite. I take a seat beside Jarny, who's all sweaty and catching his breath. The two new girls leave after one of them nearly falls over while dancing. Jasmine's already disappeared. Matt and Andy go back to their camp after a while too, and Troy turns the music down. He sits with me, Jarny, and Kalyn, and I feel like I'm falling asleep.

"What're your plans for the summer?" Troy asks.

We all shrug. "Probably just relax," Kalyn says.

Their words turn to blurs as I finish my beer. My thoughts are full of disappointment, because Levi hasn't come back. He must have just crawled into his tent and fallen asleep. I thought he'd come back. I want him to come back. Maybe he's lying in his tent, naked, waiting for me to come find him.

The thought surprises me. It's a bad thought—one I shouldn't be having. But it forces itself into life, and I don't like how effortlessly it's appeared. I shake my head and let it fade away.

"Grog's got me, boys," I say. Kalyn and Jarny stand with me, and we wave to Troy as we leave. We start off along the dirt and head up the mountain road. It's still so warm out. I'm all sweaty.

"Tesha dumped me," I say.

"Shit," Jarny replies. "You all right?"

"Yeah. I guess I kinda knew it was coming."

Kalyn just pats me on the shoulder and it's kind of nice—kind of brotherly. We stop in front of his house, and him and Jarny head inside to keep drinking and play Xbox, but I long for my pillow. I just say I'm going home and walk away.

It's annoying that I can see Tesha's house from my front yard. It all looks dark. She's probably sound asleep. Breaking up with me was probably exhausting. Maybe it was a relief for her. Maybe it is for me too.

I sneak through the front door. All the kids are asleep in front of the TV again. I step over their little bodies and switch off the TV. I climb up the stairs and I really have to concentrate.

In my bedroom, I step on Tomas's mattress before realizing I might be stepping on him too. But he's not on it—he's standing at my open window, smoking a joint. The smell hits me like cooking meat in a frying pan on an empty stomach, and he suddenly looks like a very different boy from the one who's been taking up all my space.

"Sorry," he says. "Do you mind if I smoke in here?"

"All good," I say, shutting the door behind me. The moonlight shines over his body—him in just his football shorts, leaning on my windowsill. I take a towel from my floor and press it against the bottom of the door.

"You want some?" he asks. I'm sleepy, but feeling less like shit sounds good. I unbutton my shirt and he hands me the joint.

"Where'd you get this?" I ask.

"Got a friend to roll a couple for me before I came here."

I take a drag and hand it back. He takes a drag and wheezes quietly. He sounds almost like a mouse. He takes a smaller drag and hands the joint back to me.

"You got blue eyes," he says. "I never seen a Koori with blue eyes before."

I'm too tired to really put the effort into my words. "Yeah, got it from my dad, I guess."

I bring the joint to my lips again. The butt wears the moisture he's left there on the end, from his lips. I draw back and blow the smoke out. I take another draw, and then I'm high and giggling like an idiot.

"You know *dealers*, then?" I tease.

"I didn't buy it." He chuckles. "My friend gave it to me. He had to get rid of it because his family was visiting for Christmas."

"Are you, like, a *stoner* or something?"

"Nah. Not really. But I heard it's good for creativity, so . . . thought I'd take all the help I can get." He takes another draw.

"Creativity? You a painter or something?"

"No, it's part of my *recovery* or whatever. They want me to focus on art."

"Who does?"

"The judge and shit."

"Oh."

He scrambles for his backpack near the mattress on the floor, unzips the big pocket, and pulls out a stack of papers. Handing them to me, he pulls out his phone, shining light over them. I see he has handwritten notes all over the page, like a madman, in blue pen.

"I'm part of this program for black kids, where they try to make you do artsy stuff to get out of trouble. I'm writing a graphic novel."

"What? Like a comic book?"

"No. A *graphic novel*."

"Isn't that just, like, a *long* comic book?"

He's silent for a moment, then we both chuckle. Grabbing the papers, he slides them back into his bag. Then he finishes the joint, crushes it on my windowsill, and throws the butt into the backyard. His bare feet are silent on my floor as he moves across the room.

"Your Aunty is pretty cool," he says, lowering himself onto his mattress.

"Yeah, she's all right." I take off my pants and my shirt. It's dark enough for him not to see anything. I crawl onto my bed and close my eyes. "You need another pillow or anything?"

"Nah, I'm good."

I'm surprised at myself. I just offered him another pillow . . . except I don't have another pillow to spare. I'd have had to give him mine and use nothing, or go check the storage under the stairs, which would have been a lot of effort, to go all the way down and come all the way back up again. I'm glad he said no.

Soon enough, he's snoring. No, it's not just a snore, it's a train rolling along the tracks. It's the train's engine, breaking into pieces and chugging along regardless, with such gusto. I'm less annoyed about it though. Maybe it's because I'm high. Good thing I'm passing out, so I won't have time to change my mind.

SIX

I'm up before Tomas in the morning. All the kids are in the lounge room, singing along to some kids' show I now hate more than anything. Aunty Pam greets Tomas when he arrives in the kitchen. Mum fixes him a plate of bacon and eggs.

How lovely it is that he got a nice long sleep while I had to listen to him snore all night.

He sits beside me at the table and digs into his food. Again, he chews with his mouth open, smacking and mushing the food so loudly.

"Why don't you take Tomas and the kids down to the lake? Me and Aunty want to get some painting done," Mum says.

"Today?"

"Yeah. Why? What plans you got?"

"I don't have any. But I guess it wouldn't matter if I did, eh?"

"Stop sooking around. I told you not to drink, because it turns you into a prick like your father."

I almost laugh. I like it when Mum swears, for some reason.

"Fine. But don't get pissy at me when someone gets bitten by a snake again," I say.

"You'll be right," Aunty Pam says to Tomas. "Take your books down and get some drawing done. It's important, remember?"

Tomas nods.

I head through the lounge room. "Get your swimmers," I say to the boys. "We're going to the lake."

I'm feeling quite annoyed today. Maybe it's the hangover. Maybe it's Tesha dumping me. I dunno. What I do know is: I'm in a foul mood.

Tomas beats me to the shower. I just sit on my mattress until it's my turn. I check my phone for the first time and there's a message from Tesha.

Hey, u OK?

I ignore it. It's been over ten minutes, and Tomas is still in the shower. I want to bang on the door, tell him to hurry the fuck up, but still I just sit there on my mattress. Then I send a text back to Tesha.

You don't need to check up on me.

Tomas finally finishes in the shower and waltzes into my room, towel around his waist, like he owns the place. And it's so hot and wet in the bathroom. He must have had the water on the highest temperature the whole time, scalded himself. The mirror is all foggy and the floor is slippery. The drying bathmat hangs on its post. I lay it down and turn on the shower.

When I get back to my room, Tomas is dressed in a shirt and football shorts, with flip-flops on his feet.

"I'll meet ya downstairs," he says. He's carrying a sketchbook and pencils. I slam the door shut when he leaves.

I dry myself as much as I can, but I just seem to get wetter. I put on a tank top and shorts and head downstairs.

All the boys wait on the lounge with Tomas. I'm getting sick of the sight of them. Henry jumps up when I arrive.

"All right, let's go," I say in the most monotonous tone I can muster. Outside, the other kids of the Mish are playing on their bicycles and scooters in the street. They kick footballs and run around while the dogs laze on the road.

We all walk together in a bunch. I notice Bobby still wears a Band-Aid on his ankle. Jude walks on one side of him and Henry on the other, and they remind me of me, Jarny, and Kalyn when we were younger. We were like that, always walking somewhere together.

"How far's the lake?" Tomas asks.

"Like twenty minutes," I say. I push ahead and listen to all of their flip-flops smack on the ground as they walk. I'm barefoot. My soles are hard enough to act as a cheap pair of shoes.

The sun is burning today. Ahead of us, near the toilet blocks, I see Tesha. She's with a couple of her cousins. I keep my eyes forward as we pass. I hope she doesn't look my way and see us. I hope she doesn't call out to me or anything.

As we pass Kalyn's house, the front door bursts open. "Where youse goin'?" He must have seen us from the window.

"The lake," I say. I realize I'm still a little dizzy from the hangover.

"Hold up!" he shouts. He races back inside and comes out with football shorts on and a towel in his hand. "Who's this?" he asks, pointing back at Tomas, who's walking quietly, Aunty Pam's sky-blue sunglasses over his eyes, sketchbook at his side.

"Oh, that's Tomas. He's living with Aunty Pam for a while."

Kalyn and Tomas introduce themselves to each other. I just

breathe through my annoyance at the kids racing forward and running back and shouting and laughing and teasing each other and spitting on the ground and fake farting. We reach the bottom of the hill and walk through the camping ground.

"There's my boys!" Troy shouts from his campsite, and the only thing I want in the world is for him not to join us. He shares a few words with Kalyn as I continue on with Tomas and the boys. We pass the other campers, and the tall trees neatly guiding the cleared dirt road as it maneuvers around all the small campsite clearings. The trees offer us a spread of shade and sunlight.

As we start along the pathway to the lake, my eyes are scanning for snakes. I turn back to find little Bobby, and he is scanning for snakes as well.

We arrive at the lake. Unsurprisingly, it is occupied by the white campers. They spread in numbers on the sand around the edges, and swim in the water. Their laughter is loud as they play. I'm so hungover I could probably vomit if I bent myself over.

We walk along the rim of the lake and find a spot by some shallows. We lay down our towels, and I assemble all the boys in a line and rub sunscreen on their backs and shoulders.

"I thought blackfellas don't need sunscreen," Tomas comments. I just ignore him. When I've applied the sunscreen to all the boys, they race into the water.

"Don't go too deep!" I shout. I take off my top, leave it on my towel, and follow Kalyn into the water. "Coming, Tomas?"

"Maybe later," he says as he sits down and opens his sketchbook. He's already wet, though—he has sweat all over his forehead.

The water is so cold as it rises from my ankles to my knees to my man-parts. I duck under the water, come back up, and my curls are falling over my eyes. I wipe them to the side and there's Tomas sketching on the bank.

"What's his story?" Kalyn asks. He keeps his voice quiet, but the sounds of the kids splashing each other masks us.

"Dunno, really. He's living with Aunty Pam, just got out of juvie," I say, keeping to his volume.

"Juvie? What he do?"

"Dunno. I didn't ask."

"What if he's, like, a rapist or something?"

"I don't think so," I say. But I can't be sure.

Me and Kalyn swim a bit farther towards the center of the lake, until we can't reach the bottom with our feet and have to tread water. All the camping teens turn up, gathering in a group farther down the shore: Jasmine, Matt, Andy, Levi. I'm excited to see Levi is still here, although the excitement scares me. I'm too intrigued by him.

And then I see Jarny. He's coming around the bend, standing tall on his bark canoe. He's stuck his Aboriginal flag into place, and it's swaying in the gentle breeze. He's paddling as he stands, and I feel bad because last year the three of us did that together on the canoe, but now Jarny's alone.

"Oi, white boy!" I hear him shout to the group of teens. "Where's my rent?"

"Look at this fool," Kalyn says with a laugh.

"You're on Aboriginal land," Jarny continues. I just roll my eyes, as the teens exchange words with him and he laughs before heading our way. I notice that the parents along the bank with their children have stopped to stare. Levi's staring too.

Me and Kalyn return to our towels. Tomas is slouched back on his own towel now, no longer sketching. He stares at Jarny as he approaches, paddle gliding through the water.

"Why didn't you tell us you were getting the canoe?" Kalyn asks.

"Well, I figured youse were gone to the lake without telling me, so I had to do it alone."

I didn't even think to ask Jarny if he wanted to join us. He lands the canoe and pulls it onto the sand, then introduces himself to Tomas, who introduces himself back. The kids are still playing and splashing in the water. Henry is yelling at someone, then laughing, then yelling some more.

"You related to Jackson?" I hear Jarny ask.

"Nah, just living with his Aunty for a while," Tomas replies.

"What's your story?" I ask.

"My story?"

"Why are you staying with my Aunty?" I roll over and lift myself to my elbows to face him.

"Bail conditions," he says, watching me through the sky-blue sunglasses.

Jarny bursts into laughter and so does Kalyn, but I can see he's trying not to. *Bail conditions*. Tomas takes off his shirt and walks into the water. I turn my head to one side and rest it on the towel. Through my closed eyes, I just see red. I reach for my top and drape it over my head.

I dream a strange dream, finding myself in that space between being asleep and being awake. In this dream, I am trying to walk up a staircase, but the stairs keep falling from beneath me. I run, but it doesn't matter because the stairs just keep falling. After a while, the fallen stairs grow into a pile that I find myself on top of, as it grows up to my feet. The remaining stairs, guiding the way to a door at the top, begin to fall away too. I'm stuck. I have to jump, but the courage within me is too weak.

I wake to a splash of water landing on my back. The water is so cold on my hot skin. I sit up and hear Henry's laughter as he runs through the water. My back is sunburnt—I feel it when I move, like a hard growth of skin that's just birthed itself there. I sit up and put on my tank top. The kids are all still playing in the water—cheering and laughing and screaming. Out of the corner of my eye, I see that Tomas is sketching in his book again.

"Where'd Jarny and Kalyn go?" I ask.

"Dunno. They left in the canoe about twenty minutes ago," he replies.

My head is aching. I lean forward and rub my eyes. I can hear Tomas's pencil striking the page like it is happening inside my ear.

"You drawing?" I ask.

"Nah. Writing."

I look to him and see his hand moving fast. He's licking his lips and has a tight grip on the pencil. His hands are big, I notice. The pencil looks so thin when he holds it.

"What are you writing about?"

He sighs and stops writing. "It's sorta like a superhero origin story. But I want it to be unique. And I'm a shit drawer, so I thought the weed might help. I've kinda got a story, but I dunno."

"So, you're a bit of a superhero nerd?" I tease as I lie on my back on the towel.

"No, not a nerd. An *artist*." He makes me chuckle. "I just haven't been able to really get the character right. The point of the program I'm in is to show the judge that I've put my energy into something creative, so she knows I'm getting better, that I have potential. But it's hard because I can't draw for shit. I like to write, I guess. I think I'm all right at writing." His voice sounds higher somehow.

"Well, you don't need *weed*. Maybe I can help you," I say. "With the drawings, I mean." I almost stop myself but continue. "I used to be a pretty good drawer. Maybe you just need to see your superhero as a drawing first, before you can really know who they are."

"Maybe you're right," he says. "Or maybe I just need *more* weed."

I sit up and hold out my hand. He's reluctant, but he hands me the sketchbook. I take the pencil to a blank page and start drawing some boots.

"What do they look like?" I ask.

"Who?"

"The superhero," I say. I'm becoming annoyed again, but I don't want to be.

"He's Koori," Tomas says.

"And?"

"I don't fucking know," he says with deflation in his voice as he sinks to the sand. "He's the first Koori superhero."

I can't help but giggle. I turn the pencil around and rub out the boots I've drawn. "He's Koori, so maybe he's barefoot? Like, *traditional*?"

"Yeah, barefoot. Traditional," Tomas says, sounding almost

excited now. He's sitting up again. I draw some bare feet and draw up to his thighs. "He's muscly, too," Tomas adds.

I add muscles to the legs and start on the waist. I draw a belt with a rounded center, which I cover with a small pentagon at the buckle. I sketch the body, giving him a six-pack of abs.

"Maybe just a four-pack," Tomas says. I rub out two at the bottom and sketch the outlines to his shoulders. I make his chest broad and give him pecs. "And he has a scar on his neck, from when the coppers cut his throat."

I look up from the page. *"Really?"*

"Yeah. The coppers kill him. Then he rises from the grave."

"If you say so." I sketch a slight scar, which stretches around his neck like a smile.

"And give him long hair. Like, to his shoulders."

I sketch the hair, parting it down the middle and letting it flow to the sides, messy, like he's standing in front of a pedestal fan. Then I start on his eyes. I draw them angry and add the eyebrows. I give him a puffy nose and sketch big lips. I hand the book back to Tomas. He gazes at the sketch for a moment.

Even though it's just Tomas, I feel nervous to have him examining my work. I turn my attention to Henry in the water. He is swimming out and then he's treading water. I should yell at him, but just then he starts back towards the shallows.

"Damn," Tomas says. "You're a good drawer."

"Do you know him now?" I ask.

"I think so. He lives on the Mish. There's some threat, and he has to save all the children."

"What kind of threat?"

He hums for a moment. "Not sure yet."

I feel warm. Maybe it's just the heat. Or maybe it's the slight smile he wears on his face when I glance over my shoulder to him, because I feel a different kind of warm—one that doesn't radiate from the sky.

SEVEN

I arrive home with the boys just before sunset. Mum's roasting chickens, and the smell fills the house.

"How was your day?" Aunty Pam asks Tomas. She has specks of blue and yellow paint on her forearms.

"Good," he says.

"Good. Better you hang around these fellas than your other mates. All they was doing was getting ya into trouble."

Tomas rolls his eyes and we share a look. We sit at the kitchen table and are served our plates: carved chicken with vegetables and mashed potato, all topped off with gravy. All the kids end up with gravy on their faces.

Mum and Aunty Pam wash the kids, who all stack in a line at the top of the stairs and enter the bathroom in turns. I just sit on the couch with Tomas watching *Friends* on TV. We can hardly hear because of the shower and the kids upstairs howling like maniacs, but Tomas laughs anyway.

"You watch this show much?" I ask.

"Used to." He yawns and props his legs up on the couch, the

tips of his toes grazing my thigh in the process. His touch startles me, and I bring my legs a little closer together.

"Who's your favorite character?" I ask, hoping he hasn't noticed me panicking at his touch. "Mine's Chandler. I reckon he's the funniest."

"Yeah," he says, "Chandler for me too."

His voice sounds different somehow. Maybe it's the tiredness, but his words sound lighter, just as they did last night when we were sharing a joint.

The kids boom down the stairs a few at a time when they've finished washing, leaving wet footprints on the floor as they march over to their mattresses.

"We're going to sleep now," Henry says, pointing at the couch Tomas and I are sitting on.

"I know," I say, dismissing him.

"You have to leave, so we can go to sleep."

I throw my head back and groan. "Fine," I say. I stand and poke my tongue at him.

"Mum! Jackson poked his tongue at me!"

"Stop it, you boys, before I flog youse both!" Mum shouts from upstairs. Me and Tomas make our exit, passing Mum and Aunty Pam on the stairs as we head for my room. Tomas falls onto his mattress as soon as we make it through the door.

"What a day," he says. He wriggles his shirt off and drops it on his sketchbook on the floor. I sit on the side of my bed and take off my tank top.

"You wanna smoke some more?" I ask. I've hardly finished my sentence before Tomas starts scrambling through his backpack. I roll across my bed, push the towel against the bottom of the door, and Tomas is already at the window sparking his lighter. I lean beside him against the windowsill. We're smoking together again and it feels exciting, like I'm doing something terribly naughty.

"That Jarny lad's a joker, hey?" he asks.

"Yeah. He's all right, though. Takes some getting used to."

"You notice his flag was upside down?"

"What? Was it?"

"Yeah. The red was on top, instead of the black."

"Shit. I didn't even notice. I guess the whitefellas probably wouldn't notice, either."

We giggle together for a moment.

"Kalyn's cool," he says.

"Yeah. He's my cousin. We been through a lot together."

"Yeah?" His tone's changed. It sounds almost like he's interrogating me.

"Yeah," I say as I watch him take the joint to his lips.

"Like what?"

"Just stuff." I'm blushing and I don't know why. I almost want to call him out for prying, but then the joint is done and he flicks its butt out the window. He stares at me for a moment and I hold his gaze.

"I'm fucking high," he says with a giggle. "Good night."

He falls onto his mattress and I fall back on my bed. I'm lying over my blanket and I feel the breeze as it comes in through the window. It washes over my body and cools me as it hits the sweat on my chest and stomach. I close my eyes, but they open right back up because he's snoring again. Already!

"Oi," I whisper. He doesn't respond, just keeps snoring. He's somehow gotten louder than last night. I can't even fathom how he can fall asleep so easily—it's like the moment his head hits a pillow, his brain just shuts down. Automated, like a robot.

I'm awake for what feels like hours while he's just snoring away. Eventually I have to plug in my earphones to drown out his noise, and the music puts me to sleep.

The morning heat has filled the room, and I'm all sweaty and sticky. I don't hear snoring, though. Tomas is awake on his mattress.

"You gotta go get your snoring checked out," I say as I roll off the bed, slip on my football shorts and tank. I check my phone and there's a message from Kalyn.

Abby's havin a party tonight. You comin?

I reply: *Dunno.*

I walk across the hall to the bathroom and piss for what feels like minutes.

"Jackson!"

I turn my head to see Henry standing there at the door I didn't close.

"You got one too," I tease. He can't see it anyway, but he's covered his eyes in fear.

Tomas is already in the kitchen pouring himself a bowl of cereal when I make it downstairs. He's laughing with Henry and Bobby and the other kids all stacked around the table.

"Heads up. Me and Pam are gonna have a few drinks tonight," Mum says.

"Reckon you could take me for a look around today?" Tomas asks me. "Just to get some inspiration?"

"Yeah, okay," I say. "Abby's having a party tonight. I'll take you for some *inspiration* there."

I start to think maybe it would be good to take Tomas exploring or something—maybe just a walk in the bush. I know it would take me out of my head, get my mind off Tesha. And besides, maybe spending some more time with him, just the two of us, wouldn't be so bad.

"Is Tesha going to Abby's party?" Mum asks.

"Dunno. We broke up the other day."

"What? Why? What did you do?"

"Nothing, Mum." I share a look with Tomas as I take a seat beside him with my bowl of cereal.

"Tell me you weren't sleeping around behind her back," Mum insists.

"I wasn't. It's just done, that's all." I dig into the cereal, but I can still feel her eyes on me.

"Are you okay?" she asks with a softer tone. I just nod.

A relief comes over me, because now that I've told Mum as well as Jarny and Kalyn, I don't have to talk about it anymore. I know Tesha will be at the party, though. She's always there.

The kids all plant themselves in front of the telly and watch a DVD of *The Simpsons*. I get dressed into a fresh tank and shorts. Tomas is out of clean clothes, so I lend him a white tank, which hangs loose over his body, and a clean pair of football shorts. We both walk out of the house barefoot. The road burns as we step onto it, so we walk on the grass.

"Where are we going?" Tomas asks.

"Just for a bushwalk."

We walk along the main street of the Mish, which is basically a narrow road with houses along either side and bush behind them. Aside from old houses, there's the community center and small public toilet block. Uncle Graham is outside doing his gardening. His wife, Aunty Becky, was the gardener, but since she died he's been working at it like crazy. It looks almost like the kind of garden you'd find at Buckingham Palace. He gives me a wave as we walk by. Next door, Aunty Lois and Uncle Roger are having their morning coffees and cigarettes on their front veranda.

"How's it goin', Jackson?" Aunty Lois asks.

"Good, Aunt," I say.

"Tell your mum to drop in later for a cuppa."

"I will."

Some kids are playing on the lawn of the next yard. Their little high-pitched voices annoy me, so much so that I almost don't notice that Tomas is trailing behind me. I slow my pace so he can keep up, though I hate walking unnaturally slowly.

We reach the pathway I had in mind and step onto the dirt, into the bush. The trees get taller as we walk on, and there's more space between each one. The ground is covered in fallen leaves, and wooden signs are drilled into the occasional tree, all the writing too deteriorated to read.

We arrive at the top of a set of stairs cut into the mountainside, which descend into heavy forest. The bushy trees below leave no room for sight of the ground. All we can see when we look down is green. I begin to climb down the stairs and Tomas follows.

"How does he get his powers?" I ask, mostly because the silence between us is annoying the hell out of me.

"What?"

"Your superhero. How does he get his powers?"

"I'm still figuring that one out. I was thinking when the coppers kill him, they throw his body into a polluted lake, and the waste in the water grows into his body, then he uses his powers to escape. Something like that."

"That's cool," I say.

"Yeah, I thought so."

The stairs get so steep that we have to use our hands as well as our feet to climb down. We pass the treetops and travel to the darkness covering all the bush underneath. The moisture is thick in the air.

I reach the bottom of the stairs before Tomas. It's about a two-meter drop from the last step to where I am, on the ground. I watch as he readies himself and jumps. The ground is spongy beneath my feet. It feels wet and soft. Water is running somewhere in the distance. Everything is much colder underneath the cover of the tall, towering trees.

"Be careful—snakes round here," I say as I trot ahead.

"Great."

We travel deeper into the forest until we reach a small creek. It's mostly dried up, but a small stream of water from up the mountain still races through the rocks. I cup a handful and splash it onto my face and hair. Tomas does the same. The droplets of water seem to stay whole on his hair, twinkling. He shakes his head and sprays me like a dog that's just been hosed down.

"Come," I say. "Let's follow the water."

We climb down a gully, still following the creek water. The

ground appears broken, with cracks in the dirt. I descend the broken land before Tomas, wondering what he thinks when he gazes at it. It looks like there was some sort of mudslide, or earth-avalanche, as Mum calls them, as one large chunk of land has just been ripped from the earth. The water still trickles down the rough ground.

I stop walking and wave Tomas over without looking at him. When he reaches me, I point to the ground. There is an impression in the dirt and sand. I examine it and he hunches down with me for a closer look. To Tomas, it might just look like a set of horse's hooves have kicked the ground, or a large rock resting there was moved.

"Do you believe in Doolagahs?" I ask.

"Doolagahs?"

"Yeah, like Yowies, y'know?"

"Oh, right. Like the Hairy Man?" His tone has dulled, and he sighs. "You don't believe that stuff, do you?"

"I dunno. Maybe," I say. "When I was little, we were camping down the coast. All my family down that way believe in Doolagahs. The whole family was there: Aunties, Uncles, cousins, Nan and Pop. They used to tell us stories from when they were younger, camping with the elders and that, about Doolagahs. We thought they were just trying to scare us. We were all little assholes. We laughed at 'em, called 'em silly old fellas."

Tomas takes his eyes back to the marking on the ground. He hunches down and feels it with his fingertips.

"All the cousins, we used to sleep together in my Uncle's old caravan," I continue. "He pulled everything out of it, so it was just the floor, and we put some mattresses down and all slept there. We were all little, so we fit.

"One night, it was really hot and a few of us couldn't sleep. There was probably three or four of us still awake. We always left the back door open a bit, with a net hanging down to keep the mosquitos out. There was a nice breeze coming through, and all the Uncles and Aunties were asleep in their tents. Then my cousin Erin sat up and pointed at the window. The windows were big, and they were jammed, so you couldn't open them. Erin was real quiet. She wasn't even breathing. The rest of us looked, and the glass was fogged up, like someone was breathing on it."

Tomas gazes back to me, and all other sounds of the bush drown away. It's just us, standing there.

"It was so dark, so we couldn't see anything. I remember we heard scratching on the caravan wall from the outside, like a possum or something trying to claw its way in. One of my other cousins pointed at the door—that's when we realized it was still open a little bit. We all just stayed dead quiet until the scratching stopped. Then, *bang!*"

I make sure to scream the word *bang*, and Tomas gasps the most electrifying gasp. His eyes widen and his body jolts, and it's the funniest thing I've ever seen.

"The Doolagah smashed into the caravan," I continue, "and it nearly got pushed onto its side. It was shaking like crazy. The Doolagah just kept banging. We were falling all over each other. Everyone woke up and we all started screaming. Then the banging stopped. We told the Aunts and Uncles what happened, woke them all up in the middle of the night, and we left camp the next day. Never went back."

"Right." Tomas giggles. I giggle too. I guess it does sound pretty silly. "It was probably your Uncle trying to scare ya."

"Maybe. There are so many stories about 'em, though. It's hard to believe so many different stories would all be bullshit."

"Riiiiight . . . ," Tomas says.

I start laughing—it's bursting out of me. In the laughter, I get a brilliant idea.

"Maybe instead of a villain, you could have a monster in your story," I say. "A Doolagah would be a pretty good *monster* for ya."

"Could be," Tomas says with a chuckle. He pulls out his sketchbook and turns to a page headed *Villain ideas*, where he writes *Doolagah*. I can't help but study his hands as he writes. He's bitten his fingernails short, and his grip is strong on the pencil.

"You wanna come to the party tonight?" I ask. I'm almost wishing for him to say yes.

"Yeah, all right," he says. He closes his book and I lead him along a trail through the bush. The shrubbery is heavy and pokes out over the pathway, so we need to weave to dodge the cuts and jabs. A kookaburra laughs above us, probably to another kookaburra who's staying silent.

"Holy shit," Tomas says.

He points through the bushes. There are three kangaroos just standing there, staring at us. I step closer, land on some crunchy broken leaves, and they hop away with speed.

"I've never seen them so close," Tomas says.

We keep walking and come to a post, with a faded picture of

an echidna on its top as well as some writing too worn to read anymore.

"The mob at the Land Council used to do cultural bushwalks for tourists and school groups and shit," I say. "This was one of the tours they'd do—bring them out here, and people who weren't black would learn all about our culture, and about how our people used to hunt, what plants we used to make medicine, those sorts of things. My favorite one growing up was the walk up the mountain. They'd take you right up the top, and you can see everything from up there."

"They don't do it no more?"

"Nah. Not anymore. Now there's just the men's group and the women's group. The health workers come to the community center sometimes, but that's pretty much all we got now."

We continue along the trail and head uphill. The bush grows denser still, and we have to duck and weave past branches. The pathway hasn't been properly maintained in years.

"Why did they stop doing the tours?" Tomas asks.

"I don't know, really. I guess it had to do with money."

Tomas screams at the top of his lungs and jumps past me. It scares the shit out of me. He loses his footing and I have to catch him.

"What's wrong?" I ask. Tomas wriggles free from my grip and crawls for a moment on the ground before he leaps forward along the trail.

"Fucking spider," he says. I study the branches, and there is a big fucking redback spider at the center of a web, fixed just above my head over the pathway.

"Don't worry, it's not on you." I giggle as Tomas shakes his shirt and dances like an idiot. I grip his arm to calm him down. "Chill out."

He stops and stares at my hand for a moment, becoming still. His arm is warm and sweaty under my fingers. It's a strong arm. His muscle is all firm, maybe from lifting weights in juvie, maybe from jerking off. I wonder if he's jerked off in my room when I wasn't there, or while I was sleeping . . .

I let go, because I've been holding him too long. I walk past him and continue along the pathway.

"I fucking hate spiders," Tomas says, puffing behind me.

I feel all awkward now. I feel like I might have looked at him differently for that moment I held his arm. I think he might have seen how I looked at him.

"You know, I got bitten by a funnel-web once," Tomas says. "I had to go to the hospital. They said I could've died from the venom."

"I'm glad you didn't," I say.

I think the moment has passed now, thank fuck. Tomas has forgotten all about it. Maybe I'm overthinking the whole thing. Nothing happened. Nothing at all. Maybe he was so worried about the spider that he didn't notice any look I gave him. Maybe he didn't even notice I touched him at all.

EIGHT

We arrive back at the Mish and head home. The kids are running around the backyard shooting each other with their Nerf guns and water pistols, the noise of it echoing into the kitchen where Mum and Aunty Pam sip bourbon at the table, listening to Charley Pride.

I walk to the fridge and get out the leg of ham left over from Christmas. Tomas sits down opposite Aunty Pam as I get a knife from the drawer and begin slicing. I take the half-empty loaf of bread resting on the kitchen bench and throw it to Tomas.

"Take some," I say, placing the ham on the table. He grabs two thick slices of ham and makes a sandwich. I do the same.

"Reckon you can handle a Mish party?" I ask, turning to him with a cheeky grin.

"Well, I've been to my fair share of parties," Tomas says.

"You better behave yourself," Aunty Pam says. "Don't go doin' anything stupid, yeah?"

Tomas just nods. Mum gives me the evil eye as I pour myself and Tomas a glass of bourbon each from her bottle.

"He'll be right with me," I say to Aunty Pam.

She turns to see him taking a sip from his glass and rolls her eyes. "If he gets in trouble again, it's on you, Jackson Barley."

"Grog's not my problem," Tomas says. "No need to worry." He takes another sip and screws up his face, like he's just sucked on a lemon.

I understand when I taste it, because the bourbon churns my stomach.

"Get any inspiration today, Tomas?" Aunty Pam asks.

"Yeah. Got some ideas."

Me and Tomas force ourselves through our glasses. I take a six-pack of beer from the fridge and we head to my room. Tomas drinks a beer while I draw a Doolagah in his sketchbook. It's tall and looks like a grizzly bear wearing a fur coat. Its eyes are just black spirals. I draw the hair bushy and long on its head, like flaccid spikes that flail about.

"So, the *hero* lives on the Mish," Tomas says as he writes on a sheet of paper. "He's just a normal teenager. He has a girlfriend and mates and cousins and whatever. Then one day, a few kids go missing in the bush."

He sounds so intense. I can almost hear his brain speeding as he speaks.

"He goes and looks for the kids, but the cops tell him not to interfere. So, they arrest him and cut his throat."

"Do the cops really have to cut his throat? Or kill him at all?" I ask.

"Hey, I'm just being realistic!"

"Yeah, but not all cops are racist killers."

Tomas sighs. "Fine, maybe they don't kill him. But then how does he get into the polluted lake and get his powers?"

He takes another sip of his beer while I sketch some detail into the Doolagah's feet.

"Maybe he's always had his powers," I say, "and just doesn't realize until the time comes to use them."

Tomas sits forward. His eyes beam to me. "Right, okay. That's good. Maybe he finds bones of the children at the Doolagah's den. Wait, do Doolagahs live in *dens*?"

"Sure, I dunno."

"Then he fights one and realizes he has superhuman strength. And that he can fly!"

I laugh at his excitement. I finish off the Doolagah and hand him the sketchbook.

"Dear god," he says. "It's beautiful."

"Is it scary enough?"

"Fuck yeah."

My phone vibrates on my bed—a text from Tesha. She asks if I'm going to Abby's party. I tell her I am. She doesn't respond—not that I want her to. I finish off my beer and start another.

"Should we save some for the party?" Tomas asks.

"Yeah. There'll be more there, though. We always share."

I get dressed into my maroon shirt and black jeans. Tomas changes into a shirt and shorts. We put on our shoes and head back downstairs. The kids are all watching a movie. They're all quiet and don't even notice us as we walk out the front door. I realize I'm tipsy as I land on the stepping stones and aim for the front gate, with Tomas just behind my shoulder.

The road is dark and the sky is a dark blue. It's just about nighttime now and so much cooler outside. A wind whistles through the main street of the Mish. The cuffs of my pants stop just above my ankles, leaving them bare to feel the breeze.

We walk downhill towards Abby's house, and Tomas follows me onto the dirt driveway. It sounds like a big night ahead.

"Are you even drunk?" Tomas asks.

"A little bit."

"I can't tell. You don't seem drunk."

I just smile and continue to the rusty broken gate. The party house is bright. There's a large bonfire in the backyard with a group of people standing around it, smoking cigarettes and drinking. A few of the oldies are sitting around the fire as well. The old men have long gray beards and the women have messy gray hair. They look a lot older than they are.

I spot Kalyn by the fire. He's talking to a girl, who I realize is Tesha. I stand there for a moment, with my hands resting on the gate. I wonder if I should just turn around.

"You right?" Tomas asks.

I push the gate open and we walk into the backyard. I greet all the guys with handshakes and the girls with kisses on the cheek, except for Tesha. We just exchange a *hey* and she walks away. Owen offers me a wave.

"Glad you came," Kalyn says.

"You remember Tomas?"

He looks to Tomas and nods. "How's it going?"

"All good," Tomas replies. It annoys me because that's a thing I say: *all good*.

Tesha has made her way to some girls I don't know who've set up a dance floor on the dirt under the speaker, which rests on the windowsill.

I tap Tomas on the elbow and start for the back door of the

house. The music is deafening as we walk onto the back veranda. Inside, Jarny is dancing with a bunch of girls in the living room. I don't know any of them. They must be visiting.

"Jackson! Come dance!" Jarny shouts over the music.

Fuck it. Usually I wouldn't, but fuck it. Now I'm dancing with Jarny and the girls, and I hope Tesha walks in and sees me there.

Jarny moves like an animal. I wouldn't even call what he's doing *dancing*. It's more flailing his arms about and jumping up and down. The sweat comes to my brow and armpits, and one of the girls moves closer to me. The lighting in the room is dim, so I don't get a good look at her. She dances against me, and now I'm really hoping Tesha will walk in.

I'm drunk. I realize Tomas isn't dancing with us. I walk back to the kitchen, look up the hallway, then out in the backyard, scanning the crowd of people. Tomas is sitting with Abby on the grass. She pours some tequila into a shot glass and hands it to him. He slushes it into his mouth and shakes his head.

"You all right?" Kalyn asks, appearing behind me on the veranda.

"Yeah," I say as I spot Tesha by the bonfire with another girl. "I'm just trying to decide whether to save Tommy from Abby or not."

Kalyn chuckles. "Maybe you should."

I cross the backyard to Tomas. "You right, Tommy?"

"Yeah," he replies. "Abby was just giving me some grog."

"You want a shot?" she asks, holding the bottle of tequila up to me. I decline, because Tesha eyes me across the hordes of people. She's coming over here, and I feel a nervousness in my stomach.

"Hey," she says.

"Hey."

"Can we go talk somewhere?"

I follow Tesha towards the house, turning back once to see Tomas going back to his conversation with Abby. I follow Tesha inside the house, up the hallway, and into the same bedroom we didn't have sex in a few nights ago. She sits on the bed. I close the door behind me.

"What's up?" I ask as I sit beside her.

"I think we should get back together," she says.

"What?"

She's quiet for a moment. "I miss you. I feel like I'm all alone."

"Really? But we broke up, like, two days ago."

"Yeah, I know. I just keep thinking about it, and I'm sorry." She takes my hand and holds it tight. "Please, can we get back together?"

"I dunno," I say, then her mouth is on mine. She kisses me hard. I'm still for a moment, but then I kiss her back. I place my hands on the back of her head and pull her closer. Off comes my shirt. Tesha lies back on the bed and I crawl on top of her. Her hands are on my back. It's so hot in this room. I focus on the softness and the wet of her lips on mine, the warmth of her body under me. I try to push those thoughts to my penis.

Come on, I think. *Do it, just this once.*

And then it all comes to me—I don't want to get back together. I don't want to be with Tesha. I don't think I'm even attracted to her. It's so clear to me in this moment. She's just not for me.

"What are you doing?" Tesha asks as I roll off the bed and scramble for my shirt.

"I can't. We can't get back together." I grab my shirt and slide it over my body, lift my jeans back to my waist.

"Why not?"

"Because I don't love you," I say, and I realize I've used my words like a sword. I feel their sharpness and their weight. But I just leave the bedroom, walk back up the hall. Probably the best thing to do right now is get out of here.

Out in the backyard, I can't see Tomas anywhere. And fuck me. Jarny has plugged in the microphone and is rapping along to Kanye West's "Black Skinhead."

"You right, Jackson?" Kalyn asks, approaching me with a beer in his hand.

"You seen Tomas?" I ask over Jarny's rapping.

"He went for a walk with Abby."

Great, I think. I settle at the bonfire, where Owen's in conversation with someone I don't recognize. I can't help but feel differently about Owen since his stint in Big Boys. It's like he's got this dark side to him that I never realized was there, before he went away. It scares me a little, but it's also kind of exciting.

There's a cooler on the ground beside him. I take a beer. It tastes so good when I drink it. I feel such a weight over me, but the beer relieves it somehow. I think I'm just dreading seeing Tesha again. I think about what I said to her. I thought I did love her, but I just don't anymore. Strange, it feels like I never did.

"All the mob back at your place?" Owen asks me.

"Yeah," I say, "drivin' me crazy. They just run and yell and scream. All day and night."

Owen laughs. "You were like that when you was a kid, always trying to get me to wrestle with ya. I could go for a few minutes,

75

then I'd be puffed. But you'd just keep trying to chokeslam me, even though you couldn't even reach my neck."

"True," I say. Owen heads for a piss and I want him to hurry back, so we can keep talking about how much fun I was as a kid. Then I see Tomas, walking back through the rusty gate with Abby. I walk to meet him and see there's fresh vomit on his chin.

"You right, Tommy?"

"You need to get him home, he's been spewin'," Abby says.

"Perfect," I say. I nudge Tomas's elbow and direct him to turn around. We walk back through the rusty broken gate, get to the road, and stop. Tomas bends over and vomits. When he stands back up, his eyes are watery and his nose is running.

"You all right?"

"Yeah," he says, "just a bit of a lightweight. Sorry. I didn't want to ruin your night."

"Don't be silly. You didn't. I was glad to get out of there, to be honest."

"Really? Why?" His voice slurs as he speaks.

"Just my ex."

"Your ex? I never really had a girlfriend," he says.

I'm surprised, because he's an attractive guy. He has a nice body. There's a cuteness to his face. *And* he's been in juvie. Girls like bad boys, right?

"Really? Never had a girlfriend?"

"Yeah. Never really wanted one. There were *girls*, but . . . you know?"

He stops for another vomit in the gutter. I worry that Aunty Pam will hear and get mad at me for not looking after him properly.

Tomas stands and collects himself. He wipes his mouth on his shirt, and we continue up the main street of the Mish. I walk closer to him in case I need to catch him.

"You have such a good life," Tomas says. His words are slurring even more.

"I don't, really."

"Yeah, you do. You got family, mates. You're so lucky." I hear him sniffle.

"Are you all right?"

Tomas starts to cry while we walk. It's a soft cry, but I can feel it piercing something in me. I stop him, put my hand on his shoulder, all awkward-like.

"You'll be all right," I say. "Aunty Pam will look after you. You'll finish the comic book thing and won't go back to juvie. It'll all be okay."

Tomas sniffles again and a cheeky smile comes over his face. "It's a *graphic novel*, not a comic book."

We both laugh and I give him a gentle push. We reach my front gate and walk to the front door.

We creep inside, and all the kids are sleeping. We climb up the stairs and I direct Tomas to the bathroom. He soaks a towel in the sink and wipes away the remaining vomit from his chin.

"Far out. I need to pace myself," he says. I guide him into my bedroom and he falls onto his mattress. I take off my clothes and climb onto my bed. Lying back, it feels like my mattress is massaging me.

I hear Tomas rolling around on his mattress. The springs bounce and bend beneath him. The moonlight shines through my window and lights his shoulder as he struggles to get his shirt off his body and throw it to the darkness. He lies on his back and I can see his nipples, his chest, the cluster of hairs that grow there. I see the brown of his neck, his curly hair, which spreads over his pillow.

I feel the butterflies in my stomach. They're flying around, and my heart rate is quickening. He hasn't started snoring yet. The words are begging me to let them out. They bang on the door of my lips and pull themselves from the depths of my throat.

"You awake?" I whisper.

"Yeah," he says.

The words try to push themselves out again. My stomach is twisting, and I feel it telling me that it won't let me go until I speak again.

"You don't have to sleep down there," I say. I can feel my voice trembling, like I'm a baby deer taking its first steps. "You can sleep in my bed, if you want. There's enough room."

"In your bed? *With* you?" he asks.

"Yeah. *Next* to me."

His eyes open and I can see their brown as he gazes up to me. He sits up, and it's so slow when he does so. He crawls on his knees to my bedside with his pillow in his hand. I roll away as he climbs onto my mattress and stops beside me.

"This is heaps better," he says.

He rolls onto his side. His back is darkened in shadow, but I can see the aged cuts and scars that paint his skin. I could reach out and touch them. His hair falls away from his neck, and I imagine taking my finger there, brushing the skin of his neck. He would say it tickles. I would ask if he wants me to stop and he would say no. My double mattress doesn't leave much space between us, but I realize I don't want the space. I can smell his deodorant. Through my sheet, I can feel him breathe. I want him to turn over, so I can fall asleep in his eyes.

Then he does turn over. He faces me, and I can see the white of his eyes as we just stare at each other forever in the dark. Tomas takes his hand to my face and brushes my cheek with his fingers. I feel the softness of his fingertips. We just stay still. We stare. I'm drowsy, but I don't want to close my eyes.

NINE

I wake to Tomas snoring in my face. The morning light comes through my window, and the summer heat comes with it. Tomas has covered himself with my blanket, still in my bed beside me. He wakes, stretches his arms, and cracks his neck.

"Good morning," he says.

"Morning."

We stare at each other and I feel something in my stomach—something growing there somewhere. I don't like it. I get out of bed, get dressed.

"You okay?" Tomas asks.

"Yeah," I say. I just need to leave. I go downstairs, land on the couch with Henry and the boys. They're all eating their cereal, but I'm not hungry. I receive a text from Kalyn.

The mens group goin to the lake. You comin?

Yeah, I reply.

I'll pick you up in an hour.

The floorboards creak as Tomas comes down the stairs. He glances at me when he reaches the bottom. I try not to look at him, but I give in and watch as he walks to the kitchen. He pours himself a bowl of cereal and sits down at the kitchen table with Aunty Pam, who's reading from her phone.

"What you boys up to today?" she asks.

"Dunno," Tomas replies.

"The men's group's going down to the lake, so I'm busy today," I call into the kitchen.

A day away from him. I just need a day away from him and then I'll get back to normal.

"Why don't you take Tomas down there for a look?" Mum interrupts from the sink.

"But it's the men's group," I say. "For the men in the group."

"So what? Tomas is a man, he's Koori—they won't mind."

I roll my eyes.

"I don't *have* to go," Tomas says.

I stay quiet, but I'm heating up.

"It's all right—Jackson's just in a mood," Mum says. "You'll be right with him, son."

I head upstairs and take a shower. When I get out, Tomas is waiting at the bathroom door with his towel. I walk past him, into my room, and shut the door. I stand there for a moment, until I hear the bathroom door close and the shower come on. I feel so angry and annoyed. I don't know why. It's not like me, really.

I get dressed and wait downstairs with the boys. Kalyn's truck pulls up out front. He honks his horn, and I roll my eyes again and head out the front door. Jarny's in the front passenger seat, and the two canoes are in the back.

"Tomas is coming," I say. The boys don't reply, so I turn and wait for him to come through the front door. When he steps out, he's wearing my loose white shirt and black football shorts. He tiptoes barefoot along the hot stepping stones, and all my anger and annoyance feel like they're weakening, because his legs are much longer than I'd care to notice.

I get in the back seat and Tomas gets in from the other side, resting his sketchbook on his lap. Kalyn takes off and we drive through the Mish in the direction of town. I gaze out the window, watching the kids as they race along their lawns, trying to beat us. I watch the dogs as they laze on the road, not moving for anyone. I watch the sun as it beams through the few clouds that dare grow in the sky. I watch anything that isn't Tomas.

We arrive in the town and park beside the block of public toilets.

"Want anything?" Kalyn asks.

"Just a Coke," I say, handing him some change from my pocket.

Jarny follows Kalyn and they disappear around the corner, heading up the street. There's silence between me and Tomas. I get out of the car, close the door behind me, and lean against it.

"I'm sorry about last night," he says through the open window.

"It's all right. We don't need to talk about it."

It's quiet again. I can almost hear him thinking about what to say next.

"It was pretty weird," he says. "Will you still help me with my story?"

"Yeah," I say. "All good."

We don't speak again until Kalyn and Jarny come back round the corner. Kalyn throws me a can of Coke and I get back into the truck. We spin around and head back towards the Mish. Tomas sketches on a blank page in his book, next to my drawing of the Doolagah. I think he scares me, Tomas. Maybe more than the thought of a Doolagah. Maybe in a different way.

We come into the Mish, head down the mountain, and turn into the camping ground. We pass Troy and the rest of the campers as they eat lunch. The smell of sizzling meat consumes us.

We head onto another dirt road, deeper into the bush, and come out at the other end of the lake, stopping at a rusty gate. The other cars of the men's group are already here. We all get out of the truck, and me and Jarny grab a canoe each. Tomas and Kalyn help us carry them over the fence and down to the lake water. Kalyn and Jarny climb into one and paddle away, and I'm stuck with Tomas.

"Get in," I say while the canoe is still planted on the sand. He takes a seat inside and I push the canoe into the lake. I climb into the back and take the paddle to the water.

We're quiet as we glide across the lake. In the distance, the campers are swimming about and having such fun. Their laughter carries across the water. Jarny and Kalyn also laugh in their canoe. Tomas stares down into the lake, watching the ripples and the fish as we pass over them.

"You okay?" he asks, not looking up.

"Yeah," I say, though my tone is dull and unrevealing.

After that, the only sounds between us are those of the paddle against the water, and the head of the canoe breaking through the waves as we travel. Jarny tries to splash us with his paddle, but he's too far ahead to reach us.

As we approach the bank, I see the Aboriginal men of the men's group. They're behind the trees but reveal themselves as we approach. They've brought the younger boys with them as well; they have paint on their hands and speak quietly to each other. One of the elders, Uncle Charlie, is painting the younger boys' faces; they form a line to meet him. Next to him is Uncle Rex, who I reckon must be about ninety years old now.

We land the canoe against the bank. I step out into the shallow water and Tomas does the same. I drag the canoe onto the sand and rest it by a tree, and Tomas follows me up the bank to the group.

Kalyn's already started working on a dot painting on the ground. He has a large piece of manila cardboard, and he dabs the tip of his paintbrush into the small jars of paint beside him and brings the paintbrush to the cardboard with precision, patience. Jarny is painting beside him, but it's a landscape. He applies his strokes with a smooth, steady hand.

"I been workin' on this one," I say to Tomas, pointing to a sheet of canvas resting behind a rock farther down the bank. I pull it out to show him. "I don't paint too much no more."

Tomas gazes over the canvas—the sketched outline of a turtle, surrounded by blue and black dots, with its shell at the center of the sheet.

"Wow," Tomas says. "It's nice." His voice quivers.

I kneel on the grass and grab the thin paintbrush that rests beside the rock. Taking the canvas over to Kalyn, I dip the brush into the paint beside him, take it to the canvas. I can feel Tomas watching my fingers as I press down and add to the dots around the turtle. I steady my hand and my breathing.

"Why do youse come down here?" Tomas asks. He hasn't taken a seat yet.

I look out at the rest of the men's group. They all look so comfortable, united. There's Darryl, painting the white streaks across his son's body. There's Uncle Teeter, painting his didgeridoo, which he's freshly carved from a eucalyptus tree. There's Uncle Rex, who can't do very much in his old age and doesn't talk properly anymore. He walks with a walking frame and is always wearing a nice big brown jacket. Even though he's old, I think he gains strength from the men when he comes to the group.

Keeping Uncle Rex company are the brothers Lionel and Eric, painting their own canvases at the bank with their feet resting in the water. They're the best footy players on the Mish—I remember Mum once said they reminded her of Anthony Mundine and Nathan Blacklock during their footy days. But they got a bit mixed up in the drugs and the drinking, and the stories I heard about them didn't sound too good. Then Uncle Charlie got them to come to the men's group, and they're doing all right these days, I think.

We're a big family, each of us related, familiar. Even the younger boys love being painted up and are always eager to learn their dances from Uncle Charlie, even though they get super shy sometimes.

"It's a *healing* for us," I tell Tomas. "The older ones, the younger ones. Some of us have problems with drugs, grog, family, relationships. Coming here and painting with the other boys heals us. Sometimes we go fishing and camping. It's men's business. We're out on country, on the water. We reconnect with our spirituality."

Tomas sits down beside me. "Do *you* need healing?" he asks.

"Sometimes," I reply.

Uncle Charlie calls us all to gather. We leave our paintings and come together at the bank. We sit in a circle on the sandy dirt, Tomas beside me. He edges his knee towards mine, and I can feel our hairs touching each other so slightly.

Uncle Charlie wears his buttoned blue shirt and broad-brimmed hat, which is decorated with an emu feather. He holds his bucket in front of him, which he's filled with gum leaves.

"It's been a tough year for a lot of you boys," he says. "We've lost people, we've gotten into trouble and gone through some bad times. But each of us turning up here today, that shows our strength. That shows the importance of this group, and how we must stay together and stay united. If not for us, for the little ones." He points to the younger boys, who are all painted up now. "Don't these fellas look deadly? They are our future. We need to show them the way, because our culture isn't getting any younger, but it can always get stronger."

We are all silent. We always shut up and listen to Uncle Charlie when he speaks.

"What's your name, son?" Uncle Charlie asks, turning his eyes to Tomas.

"Tomas," he says, his voice so light and croaky.

"Where you from, Tomas?"

"Penrith."

Uncle Charlie smiles. "Do you know the country where Penrith is?"

Tomas shakes his head.

"Do you know your totem?"

Tomas shakes his head again.

"When you go back to Penrith, you should spend time with your elders. I won't tell you to do it, that decision has to come from you, but you should go to your elders. You should ask them about your country and your totem. Because that is your identity. A blackfella with no identity is a lost blackfella. He don't know where he belongs."

"I don't know my elders," Tomas says. The whole group is quiet. "I don't know my mob."

"You don't know your mob?" Uncle Charlie asks.

"Nah, not really. One of my caseworkers tried to connect me with things, but I didn't care. None of that really mattered. I just wanted to have fun, then I ended up in lockup." Tomas's voice is so tender, it could break in the wind. "When I got out, they put me with Jackson's Aunty."

"She'll show you the way, Tomas," Uncle Charlie says. "You just have to ask, and when she answers, listen to her. You been in trouble, done the wrong thing, made mistakes, but that doesn't have to be who you are. We all make mistakes. It's just a part of life, and we all grow a little bit every day."

As I listen, I begin to think Uncle Charlie should write a book or something, or go on a speaking tour.

"You just have to make that decision," he continues. "You can make a better future for yourself."

Tomas doesn't respond. The rest of the group stays quiet. Uncle Charlie pulls a matchbox from his pocket. He ignites one of the matches and drops it into the bucket of gum leaves, which crackle with the fire. Smoke starts to bellow from the rim.

"Come through the smoke, Tomas," Uncle Charlie says. "Let it cleanse you of the bad spirits."

Tomas stays sitting for a moment, but stands at the encouragement of Lionel. Uncle Charlie stands to greet him in the center of the circle. He places the bucket on the ground.

"Do what I do," he says to Tomas. He uses his hands to wash the smoke over his body. Tomas imitates him, washes the smoke over himself. He walks back to his seat and smiles, though I can see he's trying not to.

"That was pretty cool," he whispers to me.

One by one, the rest of us take turns stepping through the smoke, waving it over ourselves and letting the smell sink into our skin. Then Uncle Teeter starts a little fire and we have a feed of sausage sandwiches.

Tomas yarns with some of the men. They joke around and I watch the smile on his face. It's new. It's bright and has reach—it reaches me and almost forces a smile onto *my* face at the sight of it.

As the afternoon grows late, the men begin to leave with their sons. Uncle Charlie leaves with Uncle Rex, after a private chat with Tomas.

"You lads can go ahead without us," I say to Jarny and Kalyn. "We'll stash the canoe in the bushes."

Jarny and Kalyn set off onto the lake. Tomas is quiet as he gets into our canoe. I push it into the water and climb inside. The canoe rocks back and forth, then steadies as I begin to paddle.

"Wanna just float for a while?" I ask. Tomas nods.

The air is cooler as the sun begins to lower in the sky. I stop paddling when we reach the deepest section of the lake, at the center. The water looks almost black beneath us. Tomas shifts around so he can face me.

It's so quiet on the water. So peaceful. The kids from the camping ground have gone back to their campsites and we don't hear their voices or their laughter, only the sound of the water splashing against the side of the canoe.

My heart begins to race as I catch Tomas staring at me. He takes his gaze away when I catch him, then I do the same when he looks back at me. I beg myself to muster the courage to tell him what I'm feeling as he sits so close to me. I've never been able to say those kinds of things, not even to Tesha. At the same time, I don't think I want him to know. It scares me.

I look away again. I don't want to feel that need to say something, because maybe I'm wrong. Maybe I'm so far wrong that he would hate me for feeling what I'm feeling. But at the same time, it kind of excites me. To know that another boy could feel such feelings for me, any boy, would be enough. Even if he didn't, I would smile and say everything is okay.

"You know how long you're here for?" I ask.

"Not sure. I think Aunty Pam said we'll head back to Sydney after New Year's," he says.

"So you'll leave in a few days?"

"Yeah, probably. A few days."

The silence falls between us again. I gaze at Tomas's chest as he pulls off his shirt. I look again at the hairs sprinkled on his chest, just a few, like mine. My eyes wander to his stomach. I want to trace my fingers along the trail of hair that runs from his belly button to his shorts in a perfect line.

"Did you have sex with Abby?" I ask.

"Tried." He blushes. "Couldn't get it up."

"Did you like Abby?"

"She was *different*. I dunno. I guess she didn't really do it for me."

My eyes find their way to Tomas's legs, which are bent slightly, knees facing his chest. My fucking eyes have a mind of their own. They are being mischievous, but they know I want to feel his legs, feel his legs' hairs against the palm of my hand.

Tomas turns away and looks over the water. He knows. I'm sure he knows.

"That's all right," I say.

There's a pause, and he is so still.

"Did you love her? Your ex-girlfriend?" he asks, staring directly into my eyes from behind his sunglasses.

"I dunno." I stumble on my words. "I liked her. In a way."

"In a way?"

"Yeah . . . *in a way*," I repeat, and I realize I'm speaking as though I'm reading from poetry, or studying my own words. I shrug. "People like different things in different ways . . ."

"Different ways?" he asks.

Our feet are so close on the canoe floor. I could reach out and touch him.

"Yeah, different ways."

We both burst into laughter, just for a moment. Tomas rests back. His feet brush mine as he pushes them past my legs. The sweat is growing on my skin as I lean back as well. My shoulders rest against the sides of the canoe near where they come to a point.

I see him staring above my head, then watch as his eyes descend to meet mine. He giggles and looks away. There is an unspoken set of guidelines that boys have to follow when attempting to flirt with girls, but no one's ever egged me on to flirt with a boy before. I don't know any guidelines to follow when flirting with boys.

There is only us. No one else. We are floating somewhere on the lake. Alone.

I push my foot under Tomas's leg. I rest it against the skin on the outside of his thigh, between his leg and the canoe wall. I try to stay still. His thigh is warm against my foot. He moves his foot to rest on the outside of my thigh. It feels like we're playing a game of hide-and-seek. I gently brush his skin with my big toe. I see he is trying to hide a smile.

I reach my fingers to the side of his foot and tickle. He laughs and pulls his foot away. I smile and sit up, lean forward and look at him. His mouth curls at its sides. The growing line of hair above his upper lip curls with his mouth. I want to kiss him, so I can feel that hair tickle *my* upper lip. I want to brush it with the tip of my index finger.

The sky is growing darker. The silence comes again. We're avoiding eye contact again.

"You know, I wouldn't have come down if you hadn't wanted me to." Tomas leans in.

"I wanted you to," I say.

"Really? Didn't seem like it."

"I didn't think I wanted you to. But really, I did. I just wasn't sure."

"You weren't sure?"

"No," I say, turning my gaze from Tomas. "But I know now that I wanted you to, so you could see the culture we have and didn't think we just get drunk and party on the Mish."

"I knew that already." He smiles. I see it from the corner of my eye, so I turn back to him. "I have fun with you."

I chuckle. "You have fun with me?"

"Yeah. You're different from the other boys I know."

"How?"

"You're . . . I dunno . . . just different."

The cooling breeze blows over my arms as I start paddling us again and the canoe moves through the water. Tomas catches me as I stare at him, but this time, I don't look away. I want him to see me staring.

Tomas rests his arms over the sides of the canoe and lowers his fingers into the water. He flicks a splash into my face, landing it in my eyes and laughing like a little kid who just farted in their sibling's face. I wipe the water away and splash him back with the paddle. He rests back and pushes his feet between my legs while I continue paddling. He moves his feet to my inner thighs. So gently, he brushes his toes against my skin and reaches to the cuffs of my shorts. He wears a cheeky smile as I stare at him.

"People are gonna see what you're doin', you know?"

He just shakes his head. "I don't care." He sounds so determined, still rubbing my thigh with his toes as we glide across the lake.

I ease my arms, letting the paddle rest on the side. The canoe slows its journey, and Tomas pulls his legs back, giving me room. I can feel a fire inside me. It's building and growing and I can't stop myself from doing what I'm about to do.

I pull the paddle in beside me, shuffle onto my knees, crawl to Tomas. He looks into my eyes, no blinking, as the canoe rocks. My heart races faster. The blood rushes through me. My hands are shaking. Tomas leans forward and kisses me. I press my lips against his and I kiss him back.

Time stops forever for a moment.

I pull my lips back, but Tomas grasps the back of my head and pulls me closer. We kiss again. His lips are so soft, but we kiss hard. I'm having my first kiss all over again. It could be morning, night, noon, any time of day. We could be anywhere at all. It doesn't matter. There is nothing else that matters anymore. There is just me and him.

TEN

The sun is setting over the mountain as we return to the Mish. We pass Kalyn's parked truck, Tomas staying close behind me, his bare feet smacking on the ground. We've hardly said a word to each other since we made it to the shore and stashed the canoe in the bushes.

I replay our kiss over and over in my head.

We make it through my front gate and into the house. Mum is just serving dinner, and the smell of the lamb chops and gravy invades my nose. Tomas follows me upstairs, and I turn on my phone. As Tomas gets in the shower, I go back downstairs and take a seat beside Henry at the table. He bangs his fork on the plate, anticipating his dinner.

Aunty Pam sits in the chair opposite mine, which leaves the chair next to me vacant for Tomas. I watch the staircase, waiting for him to appear. I take one of the stacked plates, fill it with two lamb chops and a bunch of vegetables, and pour gravy over it for him. Then I rest it on the table in front of the empty chair beside me. I start to eat when the kids start. They throw their food into their mouths like they're starving to death.

My phone vibrates in my pocket. I check to see a message from Kalyn.

Can I ask you a question?

No worries. Sure, I reply.

The phone doesn't make it back to my pocket before it vibrates again.

Would you mind if I asked Tesha out?

My stomach feels like it's emptied itself and my heart has stopped beating. I reread the message, then text back.

Why would you even ask that?

My whole body becomes hot and I feel like I might choke on my food as I try to swallow it. My phone vibrates and I check it again.

We been talking, and I wasn't gonna do anything.

Another message comes.

But I thought you'd be ok with it.

I start to write a reply—an angry one. Why the hell would I be okay with it? She's my fucking ex. The steam is almost puffing from my ears, like in one of those cartoons. But in the end I send him a different message.

I'll think about it.

I turn off my phone and go back to my dinner. The taste seems bland now. The gravy doesn't have the richness it did before Kalyn's texts. When Tomas comes down, I barely look at him.

After dinner, I pile on the couch with Mum and Aunty Pam, and Tomas and all the boys spread out on the mattresses while we watch *Robin Hood*—the animated one where he's a fox. Tomas goes upstairs early, but I don't want to follow him. There's some sort of strange awkwardness between us now.

I hope he doesn't expect anything more from me. It was just a weird moment. It was pretty good, but it didn't mean anything. Right?

All the kids fall asleep one by one as the movie plays on. I follow Mum and Aunty Pam upstairs when they call it a night. My bedroom door is ajar, and Tomas is on his mattress on the floor. He's on his stomach and turns to see me walk in.

"Good night," I say as I crawl onto my bed. I adjust my head until I'm comfortable on my pillow. I wait for Tomas's snores, but we are both so quiet. I can hardly hear myself breathe, let alone him.

"Are we all right?" he whispers.

"Yeah," I say.

I roll onto my side, away from him, and the moonlight shines onto my face. I close my eyes and I swear I can hear his thoughts. He wants me to ask him onto my bed. He wants me to invite him up next to me. I can feel his eyes on me, anticipating the words. But I can't say them.

I wake to Tomas's snores. I stumble out of my bedroom and downstairs to find that the boys are all gone. Mum tells me Aunty Pam has taken them for a drive.

"She's left you some money," Mum says, "to take Tomas to get some clothes in town."

I'm not rolling my eyes, but I feel like I am. I just stuff the fifty-dollar note into my pocket and dig into my Coco Pops. Tomas is still asleep when I go back to my room to get my clothes and towel for the shower.

When I'm done showering, I hear Tomas's voice. He's talking

to Mum downstairs. Maybe he's telling her we kissed. I listen for a moment in worry, but he's not outing me. He's telling her about juvie—something about boys climbing onto the roof and making it onto the news.

I go into my room and pull on some socks and shoes. I realize my blue T-shirt has a stain on its chest, right in the center, probably from spag bol. I pull it off and put on a clean tank top.

I go downstairs and Mum's started playing Charley Pride at a low volume for Tomas. It's "Someone Loves You Honey." She tells him it was playing on the cassette player in my father's car as I was being conceived, which is just fucking lovely to know. Then she sings along with the chorus while she sweeps the floor, and I want to crawl into a ball on the floor and scream.

"Aunty Pam wants me to take you clothes shopping," I say.

Tomas finishes his breakfast, rinses his bowl in the sink, and places it on the dish rack. He gives me a slight smile as he trots past, and I catch his gaze again as he starts up the stairs. Watching his long brown legs climb each step, I wonder if he's teasing me somehow.

Mum rescues me, turning up the music, drawing my attention away from Tomas's legs. She continues singing along to Charley Pride, as the skateboards and scooters roll along the road outside and the warmth of the day leaks inside through the open front door. A sweat is growing in my armpits.

I swear, nearly an hour's passed by the time Tomas comes downstairs again, dressed in *my* shirt and *my* short shorts.

"You know, we have to pay for that water," I say as he lands at the bottom of the stairs.

He just smiles.

Outside, the sun stings us. There are no clouds in the sky at all, and my skin's heating up like the lamb chops I ate last night. Tomas follows me onto the road, past the Mish kids rolling around on their skateboards and scooters. Some other kids kick a football to each other. We land at the bus stop outside the community center. It's shaded, thankfully.

Tomas sits beside me on the bench, but it feels like there's so much space between us. There's nothing I can even say to him—not that I want to, really, say anything at all. We don't need to talk.

I check my phone for the time—the bus should be along any minute—and a message appears as I stare at the screen. It's from Kalyn.

Thought about it?

I just put my phone back in my pocket and stretch my neck.

The kids rush from the road as the bus comes along the main street of the Mish. When it stops, I hand some change to the driver and Tomas follows me into the air-conditioning. There are only two people on the bus. Tomas sits a few seats from the front. I take a seat in front of him.

I can feel his eyes on the back of my neck as the bus performs a U-turn in the car park of the community center; as we drive back along the main street of the Mish; as we stop for cars at the highway turnoff. He's quiet, doesn't say anything to me, doesn't touch me. There is only the rumble of the engine as we turn onto the highway and then take the turnoff to the town.

We pass the football fields where all the workers are setting up their stage for New Year's Eve tomorrow night. They wheel their boards along the grass and pitch food tents in a row adjacent to the stage. People are setting up the rides too, from the backs of trucks.

We pass the traffic lights and the pub. The beer garden looks full, and I can hear the chatter even through the bus's closed windows. The bus stops outside the shopping center, and Tomas lets the other two people exit before he does, extra polite. I follow him off the bus.

Tomas's eyes light up as he looks around the street, like he's just set foot on a new planet. His whole body turns as he takes in the other side of the street. The post office. The computer store. The pub. The library. The convenience store. The uptown supermarket.

"Come on," I say, steering us into the shopping center. The air-con hits us right away, like a blast from a propeller.

I head to the cheapest clothing store I know of. Tomas follows me inside and roams away from me. I catch the shopkeeper gazing at him. She turns away when I catch her.

"Where are all the brands?" Tomas asks me.

"What?"

"The brands? You know, Nike, Adidas, Lacoste . . ."

"This is a cheapo shop. No big brands."

He sighs as he walks past me, heads for the exit. "Well, take me to the brands."

"Aunty Pam only gave me a fifty," I say as I rush to follow him.

"Don't worry about money," he says with a cheeky smile on his face.

Nervousness comes to my stomach. "We ain't stealing," I say.

Tomas does laps around the little shopping center, peeking into each clothing store for only a moment before leaving.

"Why do you need brands?" I ask. "What's wrong with the cheap clothes?"

"They're *cheap*." He chuckles.

But he concedes, and we come back to where we started, walking back inside the cheapo shop. I wait outside the change rooms while he tries on clothes. He comes out and asks if things look good, and I just say yes to everything. He gathers himself two shirts and three pairs of shorts, and we head for the counter. The shopkeeper hands me back ten dollars and fifty-five cents, which I load into my pocket.

"Let's get some lunch," Tomas says, and I follow him out of the shopping center and onto the street.

"There's a fish-and-chips shop this way."

I point to my left, towards the beach. We have to dodge and weave between tourists as we walk there. When we arrive, all the tables inside are taken by old white people and there are three people lined up at the counter.

"Go on, then. Make sure the fish is battered, not grilled," Tomas says, nudging me inside.

I walk to the counter and order a large box of fish and chips. It's at least twenty minutes before our order is ready. I carry it outside and place it on the table in front of Tomas, who digs in straightaway. I don't know how he's eating so fast, though, because the chips burn my fingers. We're half shaded from the sun, thanks to the outstretched shop roof.

"There are a lot of white people in this town," Tomas says. "Like, not even any Asians or Indians or anything, just white people."

I nearly laugh. It's hot as hell, but there's a nice sea breeze flowing through from the beach across the road. Sand covers the pavement beneath us. I watch as some parents cross the road with their kids and walk together down the steps to the beach, for a family dip.

"What were they doin' at the footy fields?" Tomas asks.

"They have a big thing for New Year's every year, with, like, bands and rides and stuff."

"Cool." He digs his fingers into the battered fillet of fish and guides it to his mouth with the steady precision of a sloth. "Why did you kiss me?" he asks. It catches me off guard.

"I dunno. *You* kissed *me*," I say.

He's quiet for a moment as some people pass by. "Do you like me or something?"

"No," I say, so quick to the word. "Don't worry. It was just a weird thing."

"A *weird thing*?"

"Yeah. I dunno. We don't have to talk about it." I take another chip and put it in my mouth.

"You know what would be weirder?" he asks.

"What?"

"If we kissed again."

I nearly choke on my chips. I chuckle and look across the street—anywhere but at him.

"Yeah," I say. "Would be weirder if we did it again."

"We probably shouldn't."

I turn back to him. He's looking down at our food, deciding whether to take some more fish or go for another chip.

"No, we shouldn't," I say. It feels weird to say what I've just said, like it has a dirty aftertaste of something I'm not sure

I even mean. But for the good of both of us, we shouldn't.

Tomas takes another chip to his mouth and looks up at me with his brown eyes. Some salt's been captured on his lips. On the pink of them. I turn away again, towards the stairs leading down to the beach across the road.

"Wanna go for a dip?" I ask.

Tomas nods.

We cross the street quickly, to beat the traffic coming our way. And then they appear ahead of us: the white boys from the pub, Ethan and his mates. The three of them are walking up the stairs, onto the footpath. They spot me and stop their conversation. Ethan's beard is trimmed. He's accompanied by a big gym-junkie wearing a flannel shirt, and a shirtless fella built like a brick shithouse. I never remember their names.

"G'day, fellas," Ethan says. "Where're your other boyfriends? Off to the petrol station?"

"No idea," I say. I try to keep walking, but the guy in the flannel shirt steps in front of me. Ethan's shirtless friend stands behind him, the water still fresh on his chest.

"Who's this one?" the flannel shirt guy asks, looking to Tomas.

"None of your business," Tomas says.

The white boys laugh. Tomas shapes up to the flannel guy, puffs his chest out, chin raised to look up to his eyes.

"Hope we see you and your petrol-sniffin' mates tomorrow night," Ethan says. They walk around us and laugh, egging each other on.

Tomas turns to go after them, but I grab hold of his elbow. "We can't take all of them," I whisper. "We'll get 'em later."

"Fucking losers," Tomas says under his breath. It makes me smile. Just like with Mum, I like it when Tomas swears too.

We head down the wooden stairs to the beach, hit the sand, and take off our shoes and socks. Tomas carries his bag of new clothes in one hand and his shoes in the other.

A sea of white families lines the beach. We stop behind them and drop our stuff to the sand. Tomas races for the waves. I walk behind him and watch as he dives under a big one. He might not have noticed yet, but I'm very aware we are the only blackfellas here.

The beach's floor dips real quick as I walk out through the waves, dropping deep so I can barely stand and making my heart stop. I haven't swum here for years. This has always been the *whitefella beach*, whereas the one near the Mish, near the camping ground, is the *blackfella beach*. It was just always that way, growing up.

Tomas swims out, heading towards the surfers in the distance, where the waves are bigger. I keep on too, bobbing up and down with the waves before I finally dive under the ocean water. I come back up to see Tomas freestyling inwards amid a large wave torpedoing towards me. I drop underneath and open my eyes. The wave towers over me, white and foamy. When I come back up, Tomas stands tall near the shore, facing me, water dripping from his hair. I slowly back out to sea, bobbing in the waves again, and he follows.

We attract looks from the white beachgoers, who are probably wondering why we aren't at the blackfella beach. Tomas doesn't know about the blackfella beach. I decide to let myself forget about the whole thing for a while.

We go out far enough that we can't touch the ground beneath the water. The wind howls, the water shifts around us, the waves crash at the shoreline. I can feel my heart beating faster as Tomas moves closer to me. I sort of wish we could stay out here for hours.

I splash Tomas and he splashes back, then we swim into shore, riding a wave Tomas deems to be big enough. In the shallows, he gets back up and shakes his head, spraying me with water. We walk back through the sand to our stuff, and Tomas remarks that we have no towels.

"Don't worry," I say. "The sun will dry us. We'll just follow the beach back to the Mish."

"How?"

I point along the stretch of the beach, to the end where the black and purple rocks rest. "Past those rocks, we'll come to the beach near the camping ground. Just trust me."

"Looks like a big fucking walk."

We pick up our stuff and start for the rocks. Tomas drags behind me, complaining about the sun and the heat and the warmth of the sand.

The crowd of beachgoers thins out the farther we walk up the beach, though the surfers still try out the waves all the way along. The rocks grow closer and bigger as the sun falls on us. It seems to be growing hotter with each passing hour.

"Reckon my superhero should fight sharks?" Tomas asks, puffing as he tries to keep up with me.

"What?" I say. "That's the silliest idea I ever heard."

"But wouldn't it be cool? I could work it into the story, somehow."

"How?" I stop to give him a break, sitting under the shade from a bunch of trees leaning over a nearby fence.

"Okay . . . maybe the Doolagahs drive him into the ocean, or take one of the kids into the ocean. And he kills them, but then a shark attacks him and he has to fight it off. And fight the shark's family too!" Tomas catches his breath.

"Yeah, then he can piss a rainbow and send it over the Mish to turn everyone gay," I say with a laugh.

"Well, *then* it wouldn't be so weird if we kissed again," he says back.

I smile, but it's a smile of awkwardness. "It would still be weird."

He's quiet. The waves roll to the shore and crash with a bang, then they simmer out and crash again.

"In juvie," Tomas begins, "we had our own little rooms. They weren't like prison cells, just normal rooms. My bed was all right. My pillow was good. You'd think I'd love to see something like this." He points to the water, which burns blue with the shine of the sun. "But it's scary."

"Scary?" I cradle my knees with my arms.

"This world is so big, you know? And all we'll ever see is the back of a paddy wagon." His cheeks have reddened.

"It doesn't have to be all we see," I say. "I used to get in trouble a lot. I been picked up by the same copper a few times, so he knows all about me. He usually stops me in the street if he sees me in town. Asks me what I'm doing, who I'm with. It really gets to me, sometimes, like, makes me wanna just smash everything and get as drunk as I can. But I'm trying to be stronger than that."

Tomas turns to me and I turn to him. Our faces are so close.

I know what he's thinking. I'm thinking it myself as I see his eyes flicker down to my lips.

I stand up, out of the moment, and walk back into the sun. Tomas sighs as loud as possible and follows me.

"You know," he says, "that was the perfect time to kiss without it being weird."

"Stop it." I'm fucking blushing. Hopefully, the sun can hide it from my cheeks.

ELEVEN

We reach the rocks at the end of the beach. We put on our shoes and climb over the jags and roughness, over the shucked oyster shells that stick to the rocks like tumors. The cliff shades us from above.

I sit on a big purple rock while Tomas roams around, carefully stepping on the rocks and peering into rock pools.

"There's a starfish," he says, and it takes me a moment to realize he might never have seen one in real life before.

We walk around to the blackfella beach and climb down. There are some parents far up the beach, helping their children to fly kites. Some of the campers are in the waves, ducking under and coming up. Troy's standing in the shallows with Jasmine. His muscles are so defined now. He looks like a WWE wrestler. He gives us a wave, which we return.

I lead Tomas up the wooden stairs. At the top I go for the pathway, but Tomas wanders off, walks to the cliff's edge.

"You gonna jump or something?" I ask, annoyed at him for delaying us. I want to lie down and rest my back.

He doesn't respond, though, just stares out to sea, the wind whipping his shirt and the bag in his hand. It's endless, the sea, stretching on forever until it blurs with the sky on the horizon.

"It's the same blue as your eyes," he says, in almost a whisper.

"What?"

"Your eyes are as blue as the ocean."

"You trying out poetry or something?" I tease.

"I think my superhero will have blue eyes. It's unique."

"As unique as an *Aboriginal* superhero?"

He gives me a playful push, then strides ahead along the pathway. I catch up to him and walk by his side.

"So, what happened to your dad?" he asks.

"What?"

"Your dad? You said you got your blue eyes from him, but he's not around."

"Oh. I dunno. He's somewhere else. Somewhere that's not here."

"Do you miss him?"

"Nah."

"Why not?" Tomas asks.

"He wasn't a good person. Forget it. What about your parents?"

"I see 'em every now and then."

"Every now and then?"

"Yeah, my caseworker sets up visits with 'em. They usually come, but sometimes they don't. So yeah, I see 'em every now and then. I usually don't like to talk about that stuff, but it feels okay to talk to you about it."

"Really?" I ask. It makes me feel a little special, to know he feels all right talking to me about his parents. "Is it shit? To need to have your caseworker set up a time for them to see you?"

"Yeah, especially when they don't come. But that's just the way it is."

We continue along the path. The sunlight is broken into pieces through the tops of the trees as we walk under them. They arch over us and cool us in their shade.

We stop at the rusty tap. I cup my hands and have a drink of water. Then Tomas drinks for ages, slurping like a thirsty dog.

"What do you think about your parents?" I ask.

"I dunno," he says. "I don't care."

We continue along the pathway and come out to the road. Two of the Mish dogs are running, one chasing the other, as we make our way past the houses. Some of the lawns grow long. Some of the front yards have rusty old cars resting there. Some of the old fellas sit on their front porches and give us a wave as we pass.

We surrender to the couch after dinner. Henry and Jude sit between me and Tomas, and the rest of the kids spread out on the mattresses on the floor. We watch continuous episodes of *The Simpsons* and my eyes are feeling heavy. My phone vibrates and wakes me from my near sleep. It's a message from Kalyn.

Come to mine for pre-drinks tomorrow.

I text back a *yes* and put my phone back in my pocket. Maybe he's gonna ask me for permission to ask Tesha out again, in person so I can't avoid it. Maybe I don't care so much, really. Maybe I'll let him go for it.

Tomas yawns and stands up from the couch. He shares a glance with me. "I'm heading to bed."

He creeps up the steps so slowly, it's like he's begging me to catch him, but I just continue watching cartoons with the boys. Aunty Pam comes in with paint on her forearms and orders us from the couch so she can sit down and rest her back. Mum heads to bed and Aunty Pam begins to snore less than twenty minutes later. The boys give a collective sigh as I lie beside Henry on his mattress.

I gaze to the top of the staircase. It's too dark to see, but I imagine Tomas is standing at the top, waiting for me. I want my bed, but the weirdness between us keeps me downstairs.

Henry starts to snore. I realize all the boys are asleep already. I sit up and turn off the television. The house is dark and quiet now, though the kitchen light's still on. It sprays into the walkway between the lounge room and the kitchen.

I cross the wooden floor to the tiles of the kitchen. I turn off the light and creep back to the bottom of the staircase. It looks like such a hike to get to the top. I'm feeling some kind of nervousness in my stomach as I begin to climb, step by step. My heart pounds when I reach my bedroom door, slightly ajar, because I can see Tomas's feet on the end of my bed's mattress, lit by the moonlight shining in through my window.

I push the door open and walk in. Tomas is still awake. His eyes open as I close the door. I pull off my shirt. He watches me as I drop it to the floor, his arms behind the back of his head, shoulders outstretched like brown wings.

I crawl onto my side of the bed. He turns to me as my head reaches my pillow. I lie on my side and we face each other. I'm sweating all over. He has a drowsy softness about his eyes. In the moonlight, they look almost black.

Tomas rests his palm on my cheek and tucks his fingers behind my ear. I move my hand to his face, feel the spiky growth on his chin as I guide the tip of my shaky index finger. I move to his lips and trace my finger along them. They are spongy and moist. I brush the mustache that grows above his upper lip, though it feels more like whiskers.

"That tickles," he whispers.

My mouth is dry as I move my hand to his forehead. I spread my fingers through his hair and brush it back from his face. It sparks him. His eyes move to my mouth and he leans into me. He kisses me hard. His mouth opens and our tongues meet, only for a moment. I place my hand on his chest and push him away.

"No more," I whisper.

"Why not?" he asks, catching his breath.

"I don't do *that*. We just can't."

He rolls onto his back, head back on the pillow. I watch him for a moment as he relaxes. I position myself on my back too, and now we're both facing the ceiling, which looks blue in the darkness.

"No one has to know," he whispers. "I won't tell anyone."

"*I'll* know," I say. "This is the Mish. No one does *that* here. I don't do that."

Tomas breathes fast. I feel it through the mattress. He sits up on the side of the bed. The bones of his spine show through his skin.

"Okay," he says. He stands with his pillow and walks back to his mattress. He falls onto the springs and pulls the blanket over himself. I wait to hear his snores, but they don't come. They don't come for what feels like hours.

"Are you still awake?" I whisper. There's no reply.

When I wake, Tomas is already gone. I step out of bed, onto my drawing of Tomas's superhero. He's ripped the page from his sketchbook and thrown it there.

He hates me. I don't want him to hate me.

I walk down the stairs. The kids are shouting and laughing and joking, as per usual. I find Tomas sitting at the kitchen table. He's finishing up a sketch of a new superhero beside his empty cereal bowl, which still holds some leftover milk in it. It's a skinny man whose head is too big for his body.

Through the kitchen window, I see Mum and Aunty Pam out in the backyard, on their knees, laying their paintbrushes into the canvas on the grass. I pull out a chair and sit beside Tomas. His hand is moving so hard and fast as he brings the pencil to the paper.

"What you want?" he asks, turning his eyes from the page to me.

"Nothing," I say. "Are we still cool?"

"Yeah," he says, going back to his sketching.

"You understand what I was saying last night, right?"

"Yeah," he says, and there is no more emotion in that *yeah* than in his previous *yeah*.

The day drags, and I hardly talk to Tomas at all. I have a shower and head for Kalyn's.

I'm straight, I think, as I walk along the main street of the Mish.

I'm straight.

I like girls.

I want to get married to a girl and have babies with her, start a family.

I'm straight.

I play through it all in my head—Mum finding out about me kissing a boy, the community knowing. They'd call me *the gay lad, the fruitcake.* Mum would kick me out, disown me. Henry wouldn't understand until he's older, then he would hate me too.

"You know Jackson, the gay lad?"

That's who I would be.

I arrive at Kalyn's front gate, dressed in blue shorts and a black T-shirt, white canvas shoes on my feet. It's not so hot today, though the line of sweat has still collected itself at the center of my back. Music is blasting from Kalyn's backyard. I imagine him knowing that his cousin kisses boys. He'd think of me as his "gay cousin."

"Jackson, my gay cousin."

He would hate me, because I would disgust him. I would disgust Jarny as well. Jarny would worry I checked him out whenever we went swimming together. He would worry I was attracted to him, that I'm attracted to him still, that I would look at him that way. I would be the one they would joke about getting the shampoo bottle stuck in his ass. Nothing would ever be the same.

I'm not that, I think.

I can't be that.

Not on the Mish.

TWELVE

I walk through Kalyn's gate, down the dirt driveway, and round the side of the house to the backyard. Kalyn's bulldog rushes out but calms when he realizes it's just me. His tail wags, and I bend down to pat him.

Kalyn and Jarny are laughing about something. They sit in the shade at the rounded outdoor glass table. There are two unopened beers on the table, all that's left over from a six-pack.

"Happy New Year," Kalyn says. "Where's Tommy?"

"At home," I say, taking a seat between them.

"Why didn't you bring him?" Jarny interrupts. "He's been to juvie and that."

"So?" I'm almost laughing. "He's just at home, working on his book thing."

Already, I feel Kalyn is avoiding eye contact with me. I pray he doesn't ask me about Tesha. I feel it coming, though, as Jarny walks inside to get food. There's a silence between us. It's a big silence.

"I saw those white boys yesterday—Ethan and his friends," I say.

"Yeah?"

"Yeah, in town. Reckons he'll see us tonight at the fireworks."

"Good," Kalyn says, taking a sip from his beer. "Been wanting to give them a kick in the face. Haven't been in a fight with them in years."

"Yeah, back at school. Remember?"

Kalyn smiles, his gaze drifting to the sky like he's recalling the *good old days.* "Yeah. Ethan called you a black bitch, then youse started punching on. Then I jumped in, and then the teachers tried to come between us, and you gave old McDonald a clip on the chin."

I laugh as my mind drifts to that fight. "Yeah, got him a few times. They tried to expel me for it!"

We both laugh as I open a beer.

"Let's see if we run into him tonight," Kalyn says.

Jarny returns with a roll of sausage on a plate. He sits it on the table with a loaf of bread. We each slice off a piece from the roll and make a sandwich.

"So, why you askin' me about Tesha?" I ask, biting into my sandwich. I just want to get this conversation over with, though I've caught Kalyn by surprise because he nearly chokes on his devon sandwich. Jarny smiles the most uncomfortable smile I've ever seen.

"She's your ex," Kalyn says. "I wanted to make sure it was all right with you."

I take another bite from my sandwich and another sip from my beer. "Do you think she likes you?"

"I dunno," he replies. "Maybe. But you're my cousin. You're

my brother. I won't do nothin' if you don't want me to, but she said you don't love her anymore, so I thought you would be okay with it."

He speaks so sincerely, like his voice has changed and he's just been speaking in a fake accent up until this point. He keeps his eyes to the table, head down.

"Yeah. Okay," I say.

"What you mean?"

"I don't love her. I don't know if I ever did." I surprise myself this time. "It's just weird, I guess."

"Yeah," Kalyn says, finally making eye contact with me.

"Go for it," I say, finishing my sandwich.

"You sure?"

"Yeah. Fuck it."

Jarny coughs so loud, choking on his sandwich, and we all laugh. I'm just glad we don't have to talk about it anymore.

"Can we invite Tommy tonight?" Kalyn asks.

I sigh, and it's loud enough to be over-the-top.

"He's cool," Kalyn insists.

Jarny backs him up. "Yeah. Invite him—he's mad fun. I wanna hear his juvie stories."

"Fine," I say, but the thought of seeing Tomas again makes me anxious. He's hating me, I'm sure of it.

We down a few more beers each, then make our way onto the main street of the Mish. The bus is departing the community center as the sun begins to set behind the bushes. Residents from the Mish stack the bus to its brim. They cheer to us as the bus turns around and heads for the highway.

Kalyn and Jarny wait for me outside my house while I go in.

I realize I'm quite tipsy as I walk through the front door. All the boys are in the backyard, yelling and laughing. I walk into the kitchen and it's just Mum and Aunty Pam, helping each other with their makeup. Charley Pride is playing again from the stereo.

"Is Tommy here?" I ask.

"Upstairs, I think," Mum replies.

My balance deteriorates as I climb the stairs. I use the worn railing to guide me. My bedroom door is open when I reach the top. Inside, Tomas is on his mattress, only wearing football shorts. He has one of his arms propped behind his head and his other hand is spread on his stomach.

"Hey," I say.

"Hey." It's the blandest *hey* I've ever heard.

"You wanna come into town for New Year's with me, Jarny, and Kalyn?"

"Nah," he says. "I'm good."

I walk over and sit at the foot of my bed.

"Come. Jarny and Kalyn really want you to come."

"What about you?" he asks, turning to me. "Do you want me to come?"

I almost roll my eyes, and I can hear Mum's voice in my head saying, *Don't be a sook.*

"Yeah. It'll be fun. You might even meet a nice white girl from town," I say.

"A *nice white girl?*" He snickers as he turns away from me. I realize what I've just said.

"Come on. You know we can't . . . Maybe we can both find *nice white girls* and forget about this whole thing." My voice has fallen to a near whisper.

Tomas sits up and rubs his eyes. "Fine. Maybe you're right."

He sounds almost sarcastic, and he stands and rips off his football shorts, showing me his gray underwear. My eyes are stuck on it—on the shape of his ass as he walks to his bag of clothes beside the window and rummages through it. I force myself to look away as he gets dressed, because my heart is pounding, and my palms are sweating, and something is growing in my shorts. I move to the doorway but still listen to him getting dressed, to him pulling shoes onto his feet and them thudding on the ground.

"Ready," he says. I turn back to see him dressed in a buttoned light-blue shirt with dark jean shorts that stop above his knees and show his thigh muscles and his brown skin stretching down to the ankle socks disappearing into his shoes.

I turn and head down the stairs. Tomas follows behind me after giving himself a spray of deodorant. Outside, Jarny and Kalyn greet Tomas with handshakes, and we all walk to the bus stop.

Abby, Owen, and Tesha are sitting at the stop. That worried feeling returns to my stomach as we approach them, because Tesha spots me and rolls her eyes. She's wearing her purple dress and black high heels. I was with her when she bought the whole outfit. She asked for my opinions when she came out of the change room, just as Tomas did. And I just said she looked great. Every time.

"Hey!" Kalyn shouts to them.

"Oi!" Owen calls back.

Kalyn sits down beside Tesha, and Jarny squeezes himself onto the bench beside Kalyn. I look away when Kalyn starts talking to Tesha. Turning to Tomas, I see that he's staring aimlessly across the street, his eyes drooping.

"How'd you like the smoking ceremony, brother?" Owen asks him.

Tomas turns to him, his eyes lighting up like he's just awoken from a deep sleep. "It was great," he replies. "Never felt nothin' like it."

"Yeah, Uncle Charlie's good like that."

I just listen to them all chatter among each other and stare down the main street of the Mish. Tomas only chimes in occasionally, and he's speaking quietly tonight. Jarny comes over to me, pulls his flask from his pocket, and shows me it's filled to the brim. I take a mouthful, then Tomas takes one.

Tomas screws his face up and shakes his head. "Jesus," he remarks, his face going red, which makes me giggle.

The bus shows up and everyone piles in. I let Tomas on before me. Our eyes meet for the briefest moment, but he just gives me a blank stare. It feels like he's seeing right into my soul and is so unimpressed with what he is seeing.

The girls sit together, and Kalyn sits in front of them, flinging his legs up onto the seat so he can talk to them. Jarny and Owen start to chat across the aisle, and Tomas sits in front of them. I take the seat in front of Tomas. I don't feel him staring at me, though I find myself hoping that he is. There's a strange sinking feeling within me. It threatens to find its way to my throat and eyes. I just gaze out the window. The bushes pass by in a blur of green and brown as we head onto the highway.

We all gaze across at the footy fields as we drive into town. The rides are all going full swing, with kids and teenagers making use of them, lining up under the lights, awaiting their turn. Families sit in front of the big stage, their blankets spread on the grass. A young girl sings at the microphone onstage while a man plays a guitar beside her.

The bus stops at the gates. The ice cream trucks are set up near the entrance to the field, and the girls buy one each. Through the crowd, I see that all the mob from the Mish are gathered in a group beside the fence on the far side of the field. Owen says he's going over to say hello to Uncle Teeter, and Abby follows him.

People scream as they ride on the Pendulum. They scream their loudest when they swing and stop upside down; then they come back down and go around and around. The Pendulum was always my favorite ride as a kid. It's made up of two rectangular cages, with the seats of one facing forward and the other's seats facing the opposite direction. It swings back and forth until you reach the top.

"Wanna go for a ride?" I ask Tomas as I hear Kalyn laughing with Tesha, who's just dropped her ice cream onto the ground.

"Yeah," he says.

I suggest to the group that we all go ride the Pendulum, and they agree, so we make our way through the crowd. Every person in town must be here, plus all the tourists.

"You been on this one?" I ask Tomas as we join the line.

"Nah, is it good?"

"Yeah, look at the bastard."

He chuckles, and it feels like the first time I've seen him smile in years. We watch as the ride goes around, and the people scream, and it goes around again. I look up at the lights, white and blue, decorating the cages of the Pendulum. The ride begins to slow, then comes to a stop. The people load out of their seats and one girl walks to the side and vomits.

"There's your boyfriend, Jarny," Kalyn says behind me. I see that Jasper is with a group of girls on their way to comfort the vomiting girl. He's wearing his skinny jeans and a Kylie Minogue T-shirt. I kind of want to go talk to him. I feel bad about when I last saw him, at the medical center. He didn't hear what Kalyn said, but I feel like I should go apologize for it even though I didn't say it.

The operator clicks open the gate and we climb up the stairs. Tomas follows me as I climb into a seat. He sits beside me and we strap ourselves in. I pull down the bar in front of us and lock it into place. Jasper is still with the girls beside the ride, and I need to get my mind off the shampoo bottle.

"Nervous?" I tease, turning to Tomas.

"Nah," he says, and there's still a coldness to him. I can feel it as clearly as I feel the tightness of the belt across my chest.

The operator closes the cage wall and locks it into place. We are enclosed in the Pendulum. The ride starts to sway forward, then back, then forward again. It's slow for now. The breeze blows against us, through the cage.

"Are you mad at me?" I ask, trying to keep my voice quiet.

"No," Tomas says, sounding almost annoyed.

"You sure?"

"What does it matter?"

He turns to me, and the stare is icy on his face now as the ride picks up pace. We sway forward and turn upside down. I hold the bar as I feel myself falling from my seat. Then we swing down and around and around and around. Then backwards and around again. We start to slow, and I realize I didn't even enjoy the ride. Neither did Tomas, I don't think.

The ride comes to a stop, the bar detaches itself, and we unstrap. We climb out of the cage and down the stairs. The others meet us on the grass, teasing each other for having screamed.

"I'm headin' to the toilets," I say, turning away from the group.

"Feeling sick, bruz?" Jarny teases. I just hold up my middle finger and continue walking through the crowd. I spot Mum and Aunty Pam trying to organize the boys onto a blanket they've placed on the ground, but I just continue through the crowd, hoping they won't see me.

I cross the narrow road to the toilet block. On my way back I pass by the bar, the smell of alcohol strong in the air, and consider for a moment asking someone to buy me grog. But then I remember Jarny's flask.

The night has grown darker and the lights are in full force around the field. I find the group again and go to Jarny. We take a sneaky sip each from the flask as the nine o'clock fireworks begin to light up the sky. They bang and crash above us. The sound is deafening. All the kids and their parents marvel at the sky. Tomas is staring up at the sky too. I wonder if he's ever seen fireworks before.

The show ends and the parents start to leave the field with their children, walking back to their cars and their homes as the DJ begins to play his set onstage. All the teenagers gather below, and we're no exception. I follow Owen, who's come back to us, and we lurk off to the side with Jarny, on the edge of the growing crowd. Adults are dancing here too, even the old ones.

They seem to be imitating the teens dancing in the middle.

Constable Rogers has pulled up with his partner at the entrance to the field. He stands there and watches over us. Then I see Ethan arrive with his white mates, dropping their green VB cans into the bin by the gates. They're dressed in tank tops and jeans and look as though they've just been pumping weights at the gym.

I turn to see Abby dragging Tomas to the dance floor. She pulls him through the crowd by his wrist, and Kalyn and Tesha follow. Tesha glances back and we make eye contact. I offer a half smile, which she returns. I watch as they dance within the crowd. I watch for so long.

Jarny leaves his flask with me and joins them. I'm just standing here with Owen now. I feel weak, like I have no energy. My eyes find Tomas again through the moving bodies. He's loosened himself up, swaying his arms and bopping with the beat of the music. He catches me with a glance, and he holds it there as he dances. Abby circles him, passing between us, but he's still staring at me when I find his eyes again. The sickness returns to my stomach, and I realize I'm feeling jealous, because it's Abby dancing with Tomas and not me.

I take a swig from the flask. It goes down like water now. I lose Tomas for a moment, but find him again in the crowd of dancers. He's stopped with Abby. He's kissing her. His hands are on her waist and her arms are around his neck. My heart drops and disappears as everything inside me empties. I feel the lump growing in my throat. The tears burn in my eyes and then they leak out, like I'm a stabbed waterbed.

I wipe away my tears, hoping Owen hasn't seen. My eyes find

Tomas again. He stops kissing Abby and they start to dance again. I don't understand why I'm feeling so forgotten. I pushed him away, because *I'm straight*. And it makes no sense, because straight boys don't cry over other boys.

I almost want to force myself to dance with them all, but then out of the corner of my eye I see Ethan and his mates strutting towards me.

"Oi, abo," I hear.

There it is.

Abo.

Just like that, I am no longer a person but a thing. I'm a hollow shell, emptied of blood and organs. I sink into the earth and the whole world folds over and I'm covered in it all. I'm lower than dirt. I am not human. I'm nothing but an *abo*.

"The fuck did you call me?" I say. My whole body becomes hot. My fists clench and fire roars inside me. The fire takes over me and I can no longer control what I'm about to do.

THIRTEEN

I stomp my way over to Ethan and land a punch on his chin. He grabs my collar and my shirt rips as he punches me back. I take more hits to the face as his mates join in and I'm swung around. Owen's face appears in the blur. His punches land on the back of Ethan's head, and Ethan releases me. I go for the bastard again, punch him in the chest. One of his mates tackles me to the ground. The grass burns my face when I land. I see Owen fighting the other one, then Ethan kicks me in the ribs and his friend lifts me to my feet.

Kalyn and Jarny and Tomas come from nowhere. Ethan goes for them. He punches Jarny in the mouth, then Kalyn hits him in the face. Tomas punches the guy holding me, and I wriggle from his grip and punch the guy in the face. While I'm whacking his face, Tomas punches his stomach, and the white boy goes down. Tomas kicks him once in the face, and he rolls away through the screams and the cheers I hadn't heard until now.

"Oi!" I hear. It's Constable Rogers and his partner racing for us.

I turn to Tomas. "Come on, you gotta go before the coppers get ya!"

I take his arm and pull him through the crowd. The dancers are still dancing. They knock my hand and I lose my grip on Tomas. I turn to see him jostling through the crowd for a moment, then he disappears.

I look for the fight. Constable Rogers is standing there with his partner. Everyone else is gone except for one of Ethan's mates, who cradles his jaw. Jarny and Kalyn are gone from the crowd, although Tesha and Abby are returning to the dance floor.

I make it out of the crowd and pass by the bar, across the narrow street, and past the toilet block. Hordes of people crowd the main street. I head for the beach, past the drunken adults and teenagers, past the fish-and-chips shop, and down the wooden stairs to the beach.

I'm puffing as I walk. My hands are shaking and I'm wide-awake. I follow the sand and a freezing sea breeze rolls over me. Some drunken teens have made their way down to the shore, where they splash in the shallows.

I stop for a moment and let my muscles relax. I take off my shoes and socks, walk along the shore, and let the waves roll over my feet. The light of town is bright behind me. I glance over my shoulder, to the wooden stairs, find myself hoping to see Tomas standing there. Hoping he'll see me and come down. But he's not there.

I keep moving, farther up the beach, until my legs grow weak and I drop onto the ground, roll onto my back. I let myself sink into the cold sand; close my eyes so the darkness can calm my thoughts. The sound of the waves crashing to shore is like music to me, washing into my ears. The peace is interrupted, though, by fireworks booming into the sky. The crowd from the field cheers so loudly that I can hear them from here. The fireworks explode for so long, but I don't open my eyes to see them.

I'm straight, I think.

It is wrong for me to want Tomas.

It isn't the way.

It is wrong.

I need to forget. Forget and heal myself.

Get back to the way things were before I met him.

Get back to me, to who I was, who I can still be.

It surprises me—that I'm thinking about Tomas instead of the fight I was just in. I don't even care that Kalyn is getting with Tesha anymore. I feel like I should, but I don't. It's just nothing to me. I open my eyes and the tears leak from their corners. I look to the stars in the sky. They twinkle in their numbers, together.

I stand and pick up my shoes, start for the rocks at the end of the beach. The sounds of town drown away as I move farther along, until it's just the waves I hear, crisp and clear. It soothes me.

I climb up onto the rocks. They are so dark. I could easily fall and crack open my head and die here. I move slowly, feeling my way around until I see the sand of the blackfella beach, lit by the moonlight.

I jump down and land in the water. Of course, the tide has come in. The waves are freezing against my ankles. I stumble through the current, which threatens to drag me out. I tread out of the water and onto the icy, wet sand.

There's music coming from the camping ground—Troy must be having a party with the campers. Another year, I might have walked over there, through the bush, and joined them. But Tomas is dominating my mind. I worry that he was caught by Constable Rogers, charged for the fight, and is sitting in a holding cell.

I find my way to the wooden staircase, make it to the top, and pull my phone from my pocket, using the screen to light my way along the dark pathway through the bush. Snakes come to my mind, and spiders. I walk quickly, though. I need to get home and see Tomas returned to his mattress, so I know he is safe.

I make it to the end of the pathway and come onto the main street of the Mish. The bus is at the community center. A load of people are getting off, so I stop and scan through them.

No Tomas.

I continue up the street and pass a few drunken teenagers sharing a joint in the gutter. I arrive at my house and walk inside. Mum and Aunty Pam are watching cartoons with the boys, who are all on their mattresses.

"Is Tomas home?" I ask.

"Dunno," Aunty Pam says. "Thought you'd be looking after him."

"What happened to your face?" Mum interrupts. She stands from the couch and starts for me.

"Nothing," I say. I turn and race up the stairs. I get to my bedroom door and turn on the light. Tomas is not on his mattress.

I grab my phone and text Kalyn a message.

Is Tomas with you?

Then I walk across the hall to the bathroom and check my

face in the mirror. I have a little gash underneath my eye. It's bleeding, but not much.

My phone vibrates with a reply from Kalyn.

Na. Think he went with Owen and Abby.

My heart sinks. I sit on the side of the bathtub. He's with Abby. He's done with me. He's done trying. He'll have sex with her, and then that will be that.

I'm not straight.

I'm something else.

So is he.

I walk back to my bedroom. *Tomas. Tomas. Tomas.* As I walk to my window, I picture his face, his curly brown hair, his brown eyes, his puffy cheeks. I step on the drawing I made of his super-hero, pick it up, and stare at it. It looks a little like him. I think about what I'll say to him when I see him again. So many things I want to say. *Sorry,* most of all.

"What happened?"

I almost think it's Tomas's voice, but it's Mum's. "Just a bit of a blue. Nothing to worry about."

She stays standing there, staring at me from my doorway.

"Are you okay?"

"Yeah," I say, quick to the word. "Yeah, I'm fine."

"You can talk to me, you know?" she says.

I swear, three hours pass by and she's still standing there looking at my horrific battle scar. "I know, Mum."

"Kris! Jackson!" Aunty Pam calls. Her shout startles Mum, who jumps a little. Red-and-blue lights flash into the darkness of the hallway, and when we get to the top of the stairs I see black shoes at the front doorway. Black pants follow them. It's

Constable Rogers. A woman copper stands beside him. Their eyes follow me as I come down the stairs with Mum behind me.

"Jackson Barley," Constable Rogers says as I land on the floor, "come outside for me, will ya?"

Fucking Ethan. He's told the cops on me.

FOURTEEN

Constable Rogers is standing tall outside, wearing sheer hate on his face. Me and Mum stop inside the doorway, and Mum props up her arm, holds it between me and him.

"What you want with him?" Mum asks.

"Sorry, Kris," Constable Rogers says, "I'm going to need Jackson to step outside."

Constable Rogers and the woman copper step back. Mum lowers her arm and I walk through the doorway. The ground is cold as my feet land on the cement.

"What you want?" I ask.

"Jackson Barley, at this point in time, we are placing you under arrest . . ."

"Fuck off," I say, rolling my eyes. I turn away and Constable Rogers grips my arm. I take his wrist and he shoves me. The woman copper grabs at my neck, and suddenly I'm on the grass of my front lawn, on my stomach. Everything is dark and someone's knee is driving into the center of my back.

"Get the fuck off me!"

They pull my arms as hard as they can. They bring my wrists together and lock them into handcuffs.

"Bet you're lovin' this, Rogers," I snap as they lift me to my feet. Constable Rogers shoves me forward, out my front gate. The woman copper races ahead to the back of the waiting paddy wagon. She opens the back door and pats down my pockets.

"I'll meet you at the station, son," Mum says. I turn and see her over my shoulder. I'd forgotten she was there. "Don't say anything to anyone until I get there."

She stays and watches as they load me into the back of the paddy wagon. They lock me inside and I'm almost crying.

There are no windows to see out of. I wonder if Mum is still standing there. So many times she's had to pick me up from the police station, but never before has she had to see me arrested.

The doors of the paddy wagon close and the engine starts. We move and I rock forward. I use my feet to force myself back against the wall. The tears roll from my eyes as my thoughts turn back to Tomas. I start to worry I'll never see him again. I bang my head back against the wall. Then again. Then again. My ears ring and the pain distracts me from the throbbing in my wrists, which are tight against the steel of the handcuffs.

The paddy wagon stops and the door is opened. I climb out of the back, and Constable Rogers takes my elbow and forces me to walk. We're at the back of the police station, where all the cop cars are parked.

The woman copper holds the door open for us as I'm forced inside the station. There are coppers everywhere inside. They talk and laugh, and their fingers hit keyboards as they sit at their computers.

We come to the end of the hallway and enter the holding room. Constable Rogers uncuffs me and I have a quick phone call with the legal aid. Then Constable Rogers pushes me inside one of the holding cells. The door is metal framed, with clear panes made of thick plastic rather than glass.

"Sit tight for me, mate," he says as he locks the door.

The room is lit with an icy-white light. In the cell beside me, I can hear a man through the metal dividing wall complaining about being arrested, saying he's only had one beer and is going to blow under the limit when they take him to the breathalyzer. I sit on the steel bench in the cell and watch as the copper standing behind her computer at the tall desk offers Constable Rogers some papers to sign. Then Constable Rogers heads back up the hallway and disappears around the corner.

It's cold in the holding room; they must have the air-con on full blast. I'm relieved, though, because Tomas isn't sitting in any of these cells. I lean forward to check the clock, and it's just past two a.m.

I think Tomas will worry when he comes home to find I'm not there. Or maybe he won't care at all. Maybe they'll just ship me off to juvie. For months, even. Maybe Tomas will fuck up again too, and I'll run into him at juvie. Or maybe he'll just go back to Sydney and get moved to a new family and I'll never see him again.

I lean back on the cold steel bench. An officer leads Mum into the holding room, and she looks so big and round. The sight of her brings a smile to my face.

She waits at the tall desk while the police officer who brought her in opens my cell. He leads me to the desk and orders me not to cross a line marked on the floor. He reads a document to Mum, explaining some important stuff to her, I guess. I don't listen to the words because I'm staring at my mother's face, at the freckles sprinkled across her nose, looking black on the brown of her skin. I stare at her lips, which are big and resemble mine. She doesn't look angry, though I'm sure she is. I want to apologize so badly.

"The detectives will come and interview you soon," the officer says.

They lock me back inside my holding cell and place Mum on a chair outside. I lean forward in my seat.

"Mum," I begin, speaking through some little holes in the door's plastic, "I'm sorry."

She looks at me with a comforting smile.

"I'm sorry I let you down," I say.

She stays quiet. I turn my eyes to the floor.

"Is this because of that Tomas kid? He getting you into trouble?" she asks.

"No," I say quickly. "He's good. He's trying to be good."

"You and him are getting along, yeah?"

I look up and she has her eyes on me, studying me, still with the comforting smile on her face.

"Yeah, I guess."

I sit back and the nerves begin to grow in my stomach again. I'm going to say the wrong thing. If I'm not careful, she'll figure out what's been going on in my head whenever I think of him.

"You guess?" she asks.

"Yeah. I mean, I don't even know him, really, but yeah. He's cool."

"He's different, isn't he?"

I look to Mum as she turns to the clock and rubs her eyes.

"You know," she says, leaning back in her chair, "he's had a really hard life, Tomas. I couldn't imagine putting you through what his mother put him through. I think he's had that *upbringing* hanging over him his whole life. He probably thinks that when his caseworkers and foster families look at him, all they see is that upbringing hangin' over his head too. But you see past that, don't you? You don't even see that upbringing when you look at him, do ya?"

I shake my head, wondering where she's going with this.

"You just see him as he is—the person he is when you take away all the paperwork. And that's something really special, you know? You've shown him something really good. You know what that is?" She turns to me.

"What?"

"You've shown him acceptance. Because you like him and don't treat him no different or look at him any different. He knows that. You gave him a *normal* friend. He's probably never had a normal friend before."

I lean forward, my eyes to my toes. "What if I'm not *normal*?" My voice is quiet and shaky. "What if I'm different, like him?"

I crinkle my toes and a lump comes to my throat. My whole body is shaking. I look at her and I can feel the tears readying themselves at the gates when my eyes meet hers. She leans forward and edges her face closer to the plastic between us. And suddenly I feel at ease, for the first time in what feels like forever. Maybe it wouldn't be so bad if I got with Tomas. Maybe it would be okay.

A few minutes later, Constable Rogers steps into the holding room. He unlocks my door again, brings me out of the cell, and stands me against the wall. I look up at the camera, and the officer from the desk takes a few photos of me. Now if I become famous for some reason, the magazines will unearth my mug shot, right at the height of my career, and for a moment it will be embarrassing but then everyone will say I looked my best at seventeen.

The cops take me and Mum into another room, where my fingers are dipped in ink and pressed against a sheet of paper. Then Constable Rogers takes us into yet another small room, this one with a table and chairs. We sit down and another copper comes in, wearing just a normal shirt and pants. She introduces herself as Detective Beazley.

"Do you know why you're under arrest, Jackson?" she asks. Her voice is calm and quiet, and she enunciates her words carefully.

I do know why, but I still shake my head.

"You have been charged with aggravated assault. You are alleged to have attacked the victim at the football field before midnight tonight. Do you know what I'm referring to?"

Fucking Ethan. Fucking rat.

"Yes," I say.

"Were you under the influence of any drugs or alcohol when this happened?"

"Not really. I had a couple of drinks, but I wasn't drunk."

We are escorted back to the holding room. Mum takes her place on the chair, while I sit back inside the cell. Four a.m. comes, and we're both struggling to stay awake. With each passing second, my fear of being transported to juvie grows stronger.

"He called me an abo, by the way," I say.

Mum turns to me. "The boy you hit?"

I nod.

She just smiles. "Next time, you just have to walk away. All right? Don't give them any excuse to lock you up."

I nod again and stretch out as much as I can on the bench. "Why don't you sell your paintings anymore?" I ask.

"What? My paintings?"

"Yeah, why don't you sell them anymore? That's what you want to do, isn't it?"

Mum's quiet for a moment before she lets out a sigh. "People stopped wanting my paintings," she says.

"What you mean? Rich white people love to put Aboriginal art on their walls, don't they?"

She giggles. "They like to put the *good* ones on their walls."

"I always thought yours were pretty good," I say.

Mum's gone quiet, though. Maybe I've embarrassed her. So I just lean back on the steel bench. I lean there for so long, close my eyes.

I wake when I hear keys jingling in the hallway. A policeman is walking into the holding room. He's large and round and he wears a filthy mustache. He unlocks my door, and Detective Beazley arrives behind him. She waves me over to the tall desk.

"Mr. Barley, we are releasing you on bail. You'll have to go to children's court on the fifteenth, all right? You'll need to be there by nine a.m."

I just nod, because I want nothing more than to get the fuck out of here. She hands me and Mum some paperwork and escorts us out the front of the police station. We cross the road and climb into Aunty Pam's station wagon. My eyes struggle to stay open as we drive back to the Mish.

"You get straight in the shower when we get back," Mum says.

I've never wanted a shower more. I try to read the papers I hold in my hand, but it's too dark and my eyes are too tired. My mind drifts, hoping Tomas will be on my bed when I get back. I begin wondering what it would be like to come home from work or something and fall into Tomas's arms, as if he was my wife. Maybe he could be my *husband* one day.

Aunty Pam's awake to meet us when we get home. All the boys are snoring like they don't have a care in the world or any idea I was just locked up.

"You all right, bub?" she says with a smile. Her eyes are red and struggling to stay open, just as mine are.

"He's fine," Mum interrupts. "Go shower and get some sleep."

I don't fuck around. I go straight to my room. Tomas isn't there, so I hit the shower. When I get back to my room, I want to fall onto my bed, but all the tiredness in my body dissolves away because Tomas still isn't back.

I can't just lie here. I make my way back downstairs and outside, where the pavement is cold on my bare feet. I leave the front door slightly open, and lean against the front gate. The bus is coming again—I hear its engine and then its lights shine through the street.

The bus passes by my house and comes to a halt at the community center. I look to the people coming off the bus. They are Mish residents, but no Tomas. He's not there.

I walk back to the door and sit down on the step as the bus roars past me. A party is blaring somewhere down the road and I wonder if Tomas is there, or if I missed him getting off the bus somehow. I picture Abby's hands clawing at his back. I picture him kissing her neck, and her pulling him against her.

I've sobered up, and I think I feel a hangover starting while I'm still awake. The dark sky is turning blue, and orange light is growing behind the mountains. I don't know how long I've been just sitting here, but I'm feeling sick. I go inside and back to my room. I surrender myself to my bed. Then, the front door creaks open. The floorboards creak on the staircase. My door opens and Tomas staggers inside. His face is red in the dawn light, and his hair is all messy.

"Where'd you go?" I ask.

"I was just with Owen and Abby in town. We got a ride back to her place and had a couple of drinks. I passed out on her couch somehow."

"You didn't sleep with her?"

"No." He smiles.

I get out of bed and move towards Tomas. His eyes are so tired they look like they can hardly stay open. He tilts his head to the side, watching me, and my heart is starting to race. I take a step closer to him, but he stays where he is. I step closer and closer, and then I'm in front of him and can smell the grog on his breath.

I move my hand to his and take it. I feel his palm and rub my thumb on the back of his hand. Then I put my lips to his and we kiss. His lips are dry, but I don't care. I stretch my arms around his back and pull him against me. We kiss hard, and I feel a rush of adrenaline racing through my body.

"Changed your mind?" he teases.

"I need to know if this is really me," I whisper. "But no one can know. All right?" I'm out of breath, but so is Tomas.

He kisses me again and we fall onto his mattress. I pull off his shirt and hold his body close. I feel his skin on mine and it is so hot between us. I get on top of him and we kiss harder.

He's such a good kisser, I think, as his lips massage mine. We cuddle each other on his mattress. His cheek is bruised. I brush it with my thumb, as lightly as I can, and he smiles when I do it. Then I brush his hair behind his ear and tuck it there. I trace the tips of my fingers along his collarbone, then over his shoulders and down his arm. He forces back a giggle.

"Does that tickle?" I ask, keeping my voice to a whisper.

"Yeah. But it's a good tickle."

I kiss his shoulder, his neck, and then I find his lips again. They are tired kisses now. He rests his head on my arm, like he's using it as a pillow. His closed eyes are putting me to sleep, but I want to stay awake, so I can watch him dream. He's so fucking cute.

FIFTEEN

There's a bang at the door. I wake next to Tomas and leap from his mattress.

"Youse gonna get up or what?" Mum shouts from the other side.

"Yeah, be down soon!" I yell. I feel like I've just had a heart attack.

Tomas is chuckling to himself, watching me there at the door in panic mode.

"Stop laughin'," I say, but he doesn't stop.

Tomas pulls his blanket over his face while I get dressed and head downstairs. Bacon and eggs are waiting for us at the kitchen table. Tomas comes downstairs after me and sits in the chair next to mine, so close that I feel the hairs of his leg tickling mine.

"How was your night?" Aunty Pam asks him.

"Good," Tomas replies. "Better than Jackson's."

Henry rushes into the kitchen with Bobby chasing behind him, trying to shoot him with Nerf-gun bullets. I can't wait to get out of the house and give this whole *liking a boy* thing a try.

After a shower, I ready two towels in my backpack, put on my tank top and football shorts. Tomas waits on the couch, washed and dressed in his own tank top and football shorts. I kiss Mum and Aunty Pam on the cheek and lead Tomas out into the backyard, around Mum and Aunty Pam's big covered canvas, to the wooden shed. The sting of the sun is strong. I notice Tomas brushing his hair down, probably hoping it will protect his face from the sun.

I wheel my old bike out of the shed. Attached to its rear is a small carriage with little black wheels. I grab the bike pump and fill the flat tires with air.

"For real?" Tomas asks, while I inspect the back carriage.

"It's too hot to walk. Don't worry, you'll fit in the back." I smile.

With Tomas helping me, we wheel the bike out of the backyard, following the grass round the side of the house to the road.

"Jump in," I say as I ready myself on the bike seat. Tomas climbs into the back carriage, planting his ass on the small seat, which he complains is tight around his cheeks. His legs dangle over the sides and I can't help but laugh at the sight. I pull my phone out of my pocket and take a snapshot of him sitting in the carriage as he erects his middle finger.

We ride down the main street of the Mish, full speed. I kind of feel like a little kid again—free of concern, excited. I can't even remember the last time I rode this bike. The wind blows my hair back as we take the bumpy dirt track that leads around and then down the mountain. I look back to see Tomas sticking his tongue out of his mouth like a dog, his feet dangling in the air. I've almost forgotten I was sitting in a holding cell at the police station in the early hours of the morning. I've almost forgotten I have to go to court in two weeks.

We ride down the winding track around the mountain, picking up speed. The carriage rocks behind me, but I brake to meet every turn. On the dirt road at the bottom we pass a trio of pickups, each of them honking at us and leaving us a cloud of dust to ride through. We pass the farmlands, go over the narrow river bridge, come onto the road, and stop at the public toilets by the footy fields. The toilet block walls are chipped and vandalized with graffiti.

"That one's mine," I say, pointing to a small spray on the brick wall. It's a purple *J* with a circle sprayed around it. "Did it when I was twelve."

I walk into the toilets and take a piss, splashing my face with some cool water on the way out. Tomas looks out to the footy fields. All the rides are gone now, and so is the stage. A few men dressed in orange vests walk around collecting rubbish.

I kick up the bike stand and wheel the bike across the road, with Tomas close behind me.

"You know, Tommy," I say, mimicking a university professor, "back in the olden days, we would've needed a pass to come into town."

"A pass?"

"Yeah. Uncle Charlie reckons if you were Aboriginal, you needed to get special permission to come into town, and you had to have a good reason."

We start walking across the footy fields towards the trees on the other side.

"Do you play footy here?" Tomas asks. I find my eyes persist in wandering to his football shorts.

"Here? Nah, not anymore. I played for a team in the Knockout a couple of years ago, though."

"You played in the Knockout?"

"Yeah. They go hard there. Hardest games I ever played."

I climb onto the bike and ride ahead, Tomas chasing behind me. We make it to the bushes and towering willow trees at the other side of the field. A cooling shade falls over us.

"What position did you play?" Tomas asks as I jump off the bike.

"What?"

"I said what position did you play? In the Knockout?"

"*What?*" I repeat, turning to him with a cheeky smile.

"Whatever. Forget it." He sighs.

I chuckle to myself. "I played fullback."

"Don't you have to be *fast* to play fullback?"

"Fast?" I'm insulted. "They called me *black lightning!*"

Tomas bursts into laughter. Then he starts to increase his walking speed, glancing back as he passes me.

I see what he's doing.

"Come on, then," he says.

I push the bike along faster. Tomas begins to sprint along the tree line.

"Oi!" I shout and drop the bike, chasing after him. I run as fast as I can, and I know Tomas is doing the same as my legs burn beneath me. Our bare feet beat down on the grass. I'm gaining on him. I push myself harder, faster. He reaches a telephone pole ahead and slows himself down. I jet past him as soon as he slows his pace. When I come to a stop, he's laughing to himself.

"Not fair! You got a head start!" I shout.

"Bruh," he says with a proud smile, head back, chin out, "you just got smoked."

I grab Tomas in a headlock and we laugh together, trying to catch our breath. Releasing my hold, I rest my hand on his shoulder. I want to just leave it there, because I like the feeling of his warm skin under my palm. Tomas is quick to plant a kiss on my cheek. Just a peck.

"Careful," I tease, looking around for witnesses.

Tomas raises his eyebrows, then slowly starts backing away from me, back towards the bike we've left behind. He runs for it, and I chase him. By the time we reach the bike, we're both puffing again, and Tomas just smiles at me, the cutest smile.

I pick up the bike and we continue along the tree line until the field turns into the outskirts of the racecourse. We follow the bushes and find the new dirt walking track carved out of the bushland just a year ago. Woodchips line the sides of the track, and bamboo grows to serenade the pathway. The trees stand tall around us, arching over our heads, the branches on one side of the path meeting the branches on the other side like they're kissing.

As we walk deeper into the bushland, the sound of flowing water starts up, then grows louder. The river appears and we walk onto the rocky sand. I rest the bike against a tree trunk. Tomas steps into the river. It's still shallow, reaching to the top of his knees at its deepest point.

"There's usually nothing in here during the summer," I say, pointing to the water.

I follow Tomas into the river. The water brushes against our legs, moves between us, flowing fast. I place my hand on Tomas's cheek, lean in to kiss his lips, but he pulls his head back.

"I forgot to brush my teeth," he says, blushing.

"I don't care."

I lean in again and kiss him. It is a long, hard kiss. There is a smacking between our mouths when he pulls his lips away. I look around to make sure we're alone, but there's no one else here as far as I can see in either direction.

I walk through the water and step onto the sand on the other side. The trees stretch out to shade the water in parts. Constant mounds of sand throughout the river seem to break the water apart and send the flow in different directions before it meets farther along and becomes one again.

"My Nan was born at this river," I say. I sit down on the sand, feet in the water.

"Really?" Tomas sits down beside me.

"Yeah, after her family were brought here from down south. They got kicked off the Mish for a while by the manager, so they lived on the river with some of the other mob here. Her mum wasn't allowed to give birth at the hospital, so she gave birth here. After Nan was born, they let her family back on the Mish and she grew up there, learning about God and how to clean floors and shit."

"She must've been a pretty strong woman," Tomas says.

"Yeah. Maybe your superhero got born at the river too."

"Yeah. Maybe."

The sun peeks through the treetops and warms our backs. We grow quiet for a moment, but the trees sing us a song as the branches brush against each other, high up. I rest my knee against Tomas's, and he rests his knee against mine. The breeze rolls through the air and there's a cold touch to it as it rolls across the backs of our necks.

"Do you remember the first time you saw me?" Tomas asks.

"Yeah." I chuckle. "You were carrying the bags like Aunty Pam's little servant and the boys told me you just got out of juvie."

"I thought you hated me, the way you looked at me."

I chuckle again. "Hate you? No. I was just thinking."

"What were you thinking?"

"A few things . . . Mostly how cute you were." I smile.

I worry he might notice the growing blush on my cheeks, but I think he's blushing too.

"You think I'm *cute*, huh?" Tomas teases.

"Don't push it," I say.

I edge my face to his. The tip of my nose touches the tip of his. He moves in to kiss me, but I pull away and jump up, step into the water.

"Oh, so that's how you're gonna be?"

I splash him. He tries to dodge the splash, but I get him. He stands and tackles me into the water. My head goes under and he's on top of me. I grasp his biceps, feel his strength bearing down on me. He lifts me up and brings my head out of the water. I pull him down with me and we sit there, water to our chins. The river flows against Tomas's back and pushes him against me downstream. He grabs on to my shoulders and pulls himself onto my lap. He wraps his legs around me. His arms tighten around my back. I kiss him, our faces wet, water dripping from our hair.

After what feels like hours, Tomas climbs out of the water and onto the bank. I follow him. We hang our wet tops on a tree branch that extends into the sunlight, then we lay the towels on the sand and rest on our backs.

"What did you think the first time you saw *me*?" I ask. "Apart from that I hated you."

"I thought you looked like an asshole."

His observation makes me laugh.

"Aunty Pam told me about ya, about how you were this talented artist like your mum, but I just thought you looked like an asshole."

"Jeez. Thanks."

"But you looked a bit mysterious."

"Mysterious?"

"*He was a mysterious black guy, standing there bushy-haired,*" he whispers, like he's telling a ghost story.

"And?"

"I dunno. There was just something about you."

I roll onto my side and face him. He peeks through his eyelids and those brown eyes of his look up at me.

"That night you came back home late—I think Aunty Kris said you went to the races—you took off your clothes in front of me," he says. "I was pretty high, but I think that was when I knew."

"Knew what?" I ask.

"That I had the hots for you."

Tomas smiles, closing his eyes again and blushing like a tomato that's just ripened to its full potential. I lie back on my towel. The trees continue singing above us. The flies land on my stomach but I just brush them away.

"What was it about me?" I ask. "What could possibly be so special about me?"

"I dunno. I think it was your eyes. They were so blue."

"Just my *eyes*?" I sigh, exaggerating my disappointment in his answer.

"*They add to the mystery of you*," he says in his storyteller voice, and it almost sounds like he is telling me he loves me. "But I did like your ass as well. I mean, I still do."

I look to the sky. The treetops dominate, but there are specks of blue throughout the waving leaves and branches. I close my eyes again and am so relaxed. I hear Tomas roll onto his side, and steady my breathing as he grazes the unbroken water droplets resting on the hairs of my chest with the tip of his finger. He presses down on them and rubs the water into my skin.

"What did you do? To get into juvie?" I ask.

"I was just being an idiot," Tomas says. "Stole a car with a couple of mates and copped a chase."

"*Copped a chase?*"

"The coppers were chasing us."

"Like a car chase?"

"Yeah, but not as exciting as what you see in the movies. We just headed along the highway and turned onto a street and crashed into a wall. I was in the back, though, so I didn't get hurt or anything."

He rests his open palm on the center of my chest. He skims

the surface of my skin as he moves his hand down to my stomach. He uses the tip of his finger to draw circles around my belly button. It tickles, but I force back my laughter.

"Why'd you do it?" I ask. "Why'd you steal the car with your mates?"

"I dunno. Just for fun, I guess. Something to do. I was just stupid to go along with it."

He lowers the rest of his fingers to my skin and teases the side of my stomach. My toes are curling and my legs are twitching. I clench my fists, trying not to squirm. I'm so ticklish, but I don't want him to stop.

I hold my mouth closed as tight as I can, but a laugh threatens to escape. Tomas rests his palm on my stomach, over my belly button, and I steady my breathing, relax my arms and legs. My heart is racing, and I can almost hear his racing with it. The butterflies flutter in my stomach.

I feel his eyes on me, on my face, to see my reactions, as he moves his hand down to the brim of my football shorts. He stretches his pinkie underneath the elastic waist. I keep my face frozen still. I wonder if he can see my pulse racing on my neck as he moves his hand underneath the elastic and into my shorts, into my underwear. He holds me and it feels like my stomach is churning. I fight back a smile on my face, but he still holds me. I wonder if he's ever held anyone like this before, apart from me. It's an exciting feeling as I grow hard in his hand. I feel like we're breaking the law, doing something wrong, something terribly naughty. But I don't stop him.

"What are you doing?" I ask. He uses his fingers to walk back up to my chest.

"Nothing," he says.

I rest my hand over his and hold it against my chest. I want him to feel my heartbeat, to know it is beating for him; to know we are both alive and that neither of us is dreaming.

"I wonder what your dad would say if he saw you like this," I tease.

"Dunno," Tomas says. "He'd probably just look the other way and never mention it to me. Then he'd probably stop coming to our visits. I don't know, don't care."

My heart begins to slow, and I know he can feel it.

"What would *your* dad think if he saw us?" he asks me.

"Probably knock me out, tell me to stop being a poof." I smile. "I reckon I could take him now, though."

Tomas moves his hand away from my chest and takes his fingers to my face. He brushes the resting water droplets on my forehead with his thumb, and I can't help but dwell on the thought of my dad's face. He had spiky stubble, always. Bluc eyes. Dark skin.

"He used to drink a lot," I say. I don't even know why I'm talking about him. "He'd get drunk and lose all his money at the TAB, then he'd come home and get more from Mum. He used to hit her a bit. I tried to stop him once, and he hit me too. Mum got rid of him when I was eleven and Henry was one. I haven't seen him since."

"What will you do if he comes back?" Tomas asks.

"Dunno. Probably use the kitchen knife this time."

I open my eyes and look up at Tomas. I imagine Kalyn and Jarny seeing me here on this towel, with Tomas's hands on my body. I wonder if they would hate me, if I would disgust them.

I wonder if they would still want to be my friends, if they knew how I feel when I'm with Tomas. I picture their faces, leering through the trees. I picture them shaking their heads, frowning. I picture them walking away, and me never seeing them again.

Tomas takes his hand away and rests back on his towel again. I take the sketchbook out of my backpack and open it to Tomas's drawing of his superhero. I find the pencil and sketch some details onto his face.

"What you doin'?" Tomas asks.

I glance up from the page. "Your superhero didn't look Aboriginal enough."

"Didn't he?"

I keep drawing. The pencil is loud against the page, blending with the birds and the breeze through the trees.

Tomas arches up to see the picture. "You're a better drawer than me," he says. "Can you illustrate the whole thing for me?"

"Yeah, sure." I finish adding the veins to the superhero's muscles.

I close the book and rest it back inside the backpack. I lie back on my towel, close my eyes again, and I am in heaven. I don't want to leave. It's perfect, to just be here with him at the river. I think I'm figuring this whole thing out, but I want to go further, see if I can handle it.

We get dressed and walk to the river's edge. I know where to go next. I grab the bike and wheel it to the flowing water. Tomas grabs the carriage at its rear, and we carry it over the water. We walk with the flow, downstream.

SIXTEEN

The long branches of the willow trees hang low over the river. Dragonflies buzz close to the water—close enough to get wet. I keep carrying the front of the bike, and Tomas carries the back. As I move my legs through the water, my feet sink into the sand below.

An island rests in the middle of the river. It is covered in bushes and vines, trees stretching high. The stream divides in two around the island, and Tomas follows me down the left stream. The water grows deeper, reaching up to our waists.

We stay on our path down the river, going farther and farther. The sun moves in the sky, peeking through the treetops. My legs are growing sore beneath me. I imagine Tomas's are the same. The heat leaves me with a coat of sweat on my skin, which bleeds through the white of my top.

I step out of the water and Tomas follows me onto the sand. I push the bike through the bushes, and we make our way along a dirt pathway. The bushes around us, dense and green, buzz with insects.

We come out of the bush onto a long-grassed paddock. I start through the grass, wary of hidden snakes, and spot the building ahead. It's abandoned, broken, and graffitied. As we approach, we can see the broken windows and collapsed roof.

I shove the jammed front door open and Tomas follows me inside, into a small hall. I wheel the bike along the carpet, past various doorways, to the other end of the building, where there's an open floor, like a meeting area. The carpet is ripped in places, exposing the wood underneath. There's a smell of cockroaches in the air.

I rest the bike against the wall. Tomas creeps to the window, slowly, his eyes inspecting everything he sees. He stops at the window, which is broken. Shattered glass has been swept to the corner of the room in a heap.

"This is the *old* racecourse," I say, gazing out to the paddock. "They used to race the horses out there."

Through the window, we can make out the dirt-paved racetrack circling the paddock. The grass grows over it weakly, in patches.

"We used to skip school and come here to smoke. Sometimes we'd bring girls here at night if we were in town drinking," I say.

Tomas turns around. He stares at me with his brown eyes, standing still, his face moist with the humidity of the building. My legs are trembling. I can't decipher his expression. He looks almost worried, like he's about to tell me a deep dark secret.

I think he'll turn away, but instead he takes a step closer to me. I take a step closer too. I can hear him breathing, though the silence is loud in the room and my heart is beating in my throat.

I reach for the bottom of my tank top, pull it up over my head, drop it onto the floor beside me. Tomas watches as it lands, soft and quiet. His eyes pan over me, from my bare feet to my body, to my face. It feels like it's the first time I've shown my bare chest to him. It's exciting, but my stomach is fluttering.

I find his eyes again. They are so brown, browner than I've ever seen them before. In the dark of the room, they shine to me. I see him realize what I'm doing. I can feel it in my whole body, and we are speaking to each other without even saying a word.

Tomas pulls his top over his head and drops it to the floor beside him, just as I did. A smile appears at the corner of his mouth, and one grows on my face too. I reach to my waist and Tomas's eyes follow my hands. I slide my thumbs under the elastic of my black football shorts, pull the shorts past my thighs, down my legs, and to my feet. I step out of them and they join my top. I now stand here in nothing but my black underwear.

My palms are sweating, and I'm sure Tomas's are too. Hell, my whole body is sweating. Tomas's eyes wander over my body and I stay there, waiting for him. It's his turn now. He peels his shorts down, takes them to his knees, then pulls them out from under his feet. The darkness of his skin grows lighter the farther up his legs my eyes travel.

He still has that smile threatening at the corner of his mouth. I hope he likes me, what he sees of me. I can feel the tips of my fingers shaking. I'm sure if I try to speak, my words will be broken and my voice will fail me.

The excitement is growing inside me. My face wants to wear that excitement. I try to hold it back, but the smile comes over me and I laugh. I hold my lips tight together, hide my teeth.

I place my hands on the sides of my underwear. I slide them

down my legs and then they are off. I drop them to the side with the rest of my clothes, and now I'm naked and hard again. He sees me for the first time. He sees all of me and I have nothing left to hide. Nothing.

I smile, and so does Tomas, but the smile falls from his face as he realizes it's now his turn. He looks nearly sick in the stomach as he gazes down at himself. He guides his thumbs under the light elastic of the waist of his underwear and holds them there.

"Can you turn around?" he begs.

I smile with a sigh and turn around as slow as humanly possible. He takes a deep breath and is quiet for a moment. The elastic stretches as I hear him slide the underwear down to his ankles. He steps forward, creaks the floor, out of his underwear.

"You can turn around," he whispers with a tremble in his voice.

I turn around slowly and tilt my head up. My eyes wander over his body like a fire. I am burning him. I look up to his eyes and they meet mine again. I've seen all of him now, just as he's seen all of me. The desire that comes over me is as real as the sweat rolling down between my shoulder blades.

Tomas looks away, probably scared to see my face, to see my understanding of him, my reaction to him. I'm scared too. My throat is scratchy. My chest is heavy. My heart is racing faster than it has ever raced before. I don't want to let him down. I can't bear the thought of disappointing Tomas. I just want him to tell me I'm not hideous. I want him to get inside my head and read my thoughts, so I won't have to say them.

Tomas starts to move, stepping towards me on the creaky floor. His breath lands on my cheek. Our eyes meet again. He smiles at me. His smile isn't cheeky or scared anymore—it is warm, it is accepting, understanding, loving. He reaches out and takes my palm as he stands in front of me. His breath feels like wind in my hair.

I close my eyes, trembling. I could crumble like a stale cake as Tomas wraps his arms around me, pulls me against his chest. I can feel his heartbeat again. It calms me, knowing his heart is beating just as fast as mine. Our skin sticks together in the humidity. I feel the warmth of his armpits on the top of my shoulders.

I look up into his eyes, his beautiful brown eyes. He rests his hand on the blush of my cheek. His thumb is moist as it caresses the blackened skin below my eye. He lowers his forehead onto mine and leaves it there. He gently brushes the tip of my nose with his. I can't believe this is happening.

"You're beautiful," I whisper. Tomas presses his lips against mine and kisses me so soft, so tender. We kiss for so long standing there.

We spread our towels beside each other on the carpet to make an improvised blanket. Then we are on it, kissing hard and sweating on each other. The spiky hairs of his face are stabbing my cheeks and chin. He grabs my hair, pulls me on top of him, and wraps his legs around my waist and we are both so hard.

This is it, I think. *This is everything.*

SEVENTEEN

I'm breathless as I roll off Tomas and onto the carpet.

"Sorry," I say.

We were hardly getting started, then I ruined it. I was too quick, like a damned thirteen-year-old watching porn for the first time with his hands on himself.

"It's all right," Tomas assures me. He walks to my backpack and pulls out his sketchbook. He rips a blank page out and wipes away the mess I made. He rips another page out and hands it to me. I just wipe it all away. I just want the floor to eat me up, so I don't have to look into Tomas's eyes and see the disappointment.

"You're cute," he says, but I just feel so let down by myself.

We get dressed and leave the old racecourse building. I don't even look at Tomas as we walk the bike back through the long grass and carry it along the river.

"Don't worry about it," he says. "It coulda happened to me too."

I stay quiet. He can see my shame. I know he can. But he still smiles at me. And it's a new smile, one I haven't seen him use before. He splashes me as we travel through the river water again, and I splash him back.

We walk back through the bush and over the narrow bridge. We start riding along the road, past the farmland. The cows stare at us as we pass, and there's a thick smell of shit in the air.

"When did you realize you might like boys?" Tomas asks, and I'm glad. Anything to take my mind off my mistake from earlier.

"Dunno. I think when I was twelve," I say. "Started checking out boys at the swimming carnival at school. But I never really thought much of it. I thought it was just a phase. You?"

"One of the foster families I lived with," he says, "they had an older son. Probably eighteen or nineteen. He was a soccer player and had so many muscles. He would walk around in his footy shorts all the time, sweaty after training."

"Yeah? You do anything about it?"

"No, I was, like, ten." He chuckles. "I knew for sure that I liked boys when I was in high school. There was this boy I liked, and I tried something . . . Anyway, it turned out he was straight. I got in trouble a lot and, after that, ran away from home. I was doing stupid shit with my mates, and it just got stupider and stupider. I thought it was helping me. But the judge said this would be my last chance, so I guess I need to stop."

There is a sadness in his words. They stretch out and strain, like he's been wanting to say them for as long as he's been alive.

"I started getting in trouble too," I say. "When I was twelve or thirteen, I started getting in fights at school. Mostly because of racist shit, but I hated that I might like boys, too. I hated myself whenever I thought about a boy or looked at one in that way."

"Reckon we're the same?" Tomas turns to me with a glint in his eye.

"Maybe." I smile, and we continue past the farms. There's a tractor in the distance, going through the grass. "I sort of just decided I was always gonna be a straight guy. You know—get a wife and kids and all that. Then you came along and fucked all that up."

Tomas laughs, and I laugh with him.

"I guess we're both fucked," he says, and we both laugh harder.

We continue onto the dirt track and uphill through the bush. Instead of heading back to the Mish, though, we veer off the track towards the camping ground. Music plays loudly through the bushes, and I'm sure before we even get there that it's coming from Troy's campsite.

"You haven't properly met the campers, have you?" I ask.

Tomas shakes his head.

"They come here every year. We know 'em too well." I stop and point through the bushes. "Wanna go for a look?"

"Will they give us grog?" he asks.

I shrug and head towards the noise, Tomas following behind me. Troy's cooking some sausages over the fire, and sure enough the music is his and the others are there too. He spots us as we duck under his fairy lights.

"Fellas," he says. "What a surprise."

"This is Tomas," I say. He gives the campers a wave.

"Hey, Tomas," Troy, Jasmine, Matt, and Andy all say collectively.

"Youse want a beer?" Troy asks.

We both nod and take a seat in some of his camping chairs.

Troy brings us a beer each from his cooler. Matt and Andy go back to their conversation with Jasmine, and Levi comes over with his own camping chair and props himself beside Tomas. He holds out his hand and Tomas shakes it. The excitement comes over me easily again at the sight of Levi.

"Nice to meet ya," he says. "I'm Levi."

"Nice to meet ya."

"Do you live in the village with Jackson?"

"Nah, just visiting," he says. *Just visiting.* It hits me like a stab in the heart. I've forgotten Tomas is only here temporarily.

"What happened to your face?" Troy asks, pointing to my black eye.

"Had a bit of a fight last night," I say. "Just some racist lads from town called me an abo."

"Abo? I thought that was just a short way of saying Aboriginal," Troy says.

I roll my eyes. "No, it's racist. He may as well have called me a monkey."

"Aw, really? Well, fuck 'em, then. Wish I was there for ya."

I smile. That's probably the nicest thing Troy's ever said to me.

Me and Tomas breeze through our first beers and Troy gives us more. He drops the cooler beside us and tells us to help ourselves.

Troy's father comes out of his campervan and he looks like a true-blue, stereotypical bogan. He has a hard-worked beer belly, which he covers with a torn blue tank, and his short football shorts highlight his hairy white legs, which clearly don't see much sun.

"Hey, mate," Troy's father says as he gives me a thumbs-up,

which I return. I realize this is probably the first time I've ever given a thumbs-up to anyone for any reason. I quickly drop my hand back to my lap.

The sun goes down and a few other teenagers gravitate to Troy's camp. We have a feed of sausages, and Tomas winds up with a little bit of tomato sauce at the corner of his mouth. I wait for a moment when no one's looking at us, then take my thumb and wipe it away.

Troy puts on pop music and the campsite turns into a dance floor again. Jasmine drags Tomas up to dance. I watch from my seat as he sways his arms at his sides for a moment, then turns to me and bursts into laughter. He shakes his head and looks to the sky, as if to ask: *Why am I doing this?*

I don't even know what this music is, because I spend so much of my time listening to old-school rap and hip-hop with Kalyn and Jarny. This music we're listening to now is about as far from Biggie Smalls as you can get.

Troy cuts the music and grabs his towel, and we walk as a group behind him as he leads us to the lake. Tomas brushes my hand and I am so tempted to hold his, like we're a couple or something. He looks to me with a teasing narrowing of his eyes and a smile at the corner of his mouth.

All the white teenagers discard their clothes to the sand and parade into the water in their underwear.

"Don't go too far out!" Troy calls to everyone, as if he's our lifeguard or something.

Tomas drops his top and his shorts. He wades into the lake water and dives under. I do the same, and the night air is still warm, but the water is freezing. I follow Tomas as he swims out and treads water, swimming through the black to reach him.

"You're too drunk to be going out this far," I tease.

"*You're* too drunk," he says as he splashes me. He laughs and swims even farther out. I follow him, keeping to a doggy paddle. The teens scream and shout behind us, splashing each other. I ignore them and go for Tomas, who's gotten to the other side of the lake and is resting against the weeds that poke through the sand on the bank.

I feel the bottom of the lake rising as I near Tomas. He stares into my eyes as I approach.

"That Levi kid is gay," Tomas whispers.

"You reckon?"

"Yeah, he must be."

I can't help it. I kiss Tomas on the lips. He's all wet. His hands find their way to my back and he pulls me hard against him. The campers might see, but right now I don't care. I just kiss him. We stop and catch our breath, then we kiss again.

"I want you," he whispers.

I kiss him again. "I'm too drunk," I reply.

"I don't care," he says. He grabs my underwear under the water and I'm already hard. He reaches his hand inside, and I reach inside his underwear too. He's bigger than me, I think, but just as hard as I am.

"Wait," I say, taking my hand away.

"What?"

"I want to do it properly," I say, keeping my voice to a whisper.

"What you mean?"

I take a breath and force the words out of my mouth. "I haven't had sex before."

"Not even with a girl?"

"No. I tried, but I couldn't. I'm sort of nervous. I just want to do it right."

"Tomorrow?" he asks.

I nod and he kisses me again. He moves past me, and I swim with him back across the lake. We reach the other side and get out, leaving all the campers swimming in the shallows.

"See you, boys," Troy says, looking up from his phone as he sips a beer on the sand.

The Mish is dark and quiet. The dogs sleep on the grass as we walk along the main street. Tomas walks beside me and the carriage rattles behind the bike. We make it home and, to my surprise, no one is asleep yet. I can hear the guitar strumming away in the backyard. I want to just go upstairs and fall on my mattress, but Tomas waves me to follow him out back.

Mum has a little bonfire burning in the middle of the yard. She and Aunty Pam sit side by side on a pair of milk crates. Across the fire, all the boys sit in a semicircle facing them, cross-legged on sheets laid out over the grass. Aunty Pam is playing "Love Me Tender" on the guitar, and Mum is singing.

Tomas sits beside Henry and crosses his legs too. I roll my eyes, because I just want to go upstairs and kiss him again, but I drop my ass behind Tomas and Henry and lean back, let my elbows support me. My head is spinning a little. I notice Mum and Aunty Pam's artwork resting against the fence in the dark. It's hard to make out the picture, but they both still have paint on their hands as they put on their show for us.

Maybe I'm just drunk, or tired, but Mum's voice sounds so good. Her voice is smooth and her pitch is flawless. Her face looks lighter somehow. Maybe it's just the flickering light of the bonfire, but she looks as though she's glowing. She finishes the lyrics, but Aunty Pam continues strumming.

"Any requests?" Aunty Pam asks.

"'Big Red Car,'" Jude cries out. I nearly burst into laughter and choke on my own spit.

"I don't know 'Big Red Car,' sweetie," Aunty Pam says with a giggle.

"Do another Elvis song," Tomas says. Aunty Pam nods and starts to strum again. I don't recognize it at first, but as soon as Mum starts singing, I know it's "The Wonder of You."

I close my eyes for a moment. I could fall asleep, but I want to hear. Mum's voice sounds even better with this song. She's really good. She could have been a real singer, like a professional one who performs in pubs and clubs, and she could have gotten her first song played on Koori Radio or Triple J. Aunty Pam sings along at moments in the song, and their voices together sound like some magical Aboriginal choir. I wish I'd known this. I mean, I knew Mum liked to sing, but I didn't know she was so good. Maybe I never really listened.

When they finish their backyard concert, Mum and Aunty Pam put the boys to sleep in the lounge room. Tomas follows me up the stairs and into my room. We both crawl onto my bed and lie beside each other.

"I think I got my story all figured out," he says.

"What's the story?" I ask.

"This guy lives on the Mish. Just a normal guy. Kids start to go missing from the Mish, so he goes looking for them. He finds the Doolagahs in the bush, then fights them. They kill him, but he comes back to life with all his new powers. He goes back to the Mish, where all the town's being killed by the Doolagahs. The government decides it's going to blow up the Mish to stop the Doolagahs from killing the rest of the country, but we know they're really doing it because they don't care about black people."

He makes me laugh.

"He kills some Doolagahs, and the town is mostly evacuated, but a bunch of kids are stuck at the community center, so he goes to them. The town starts exploding, but he flies them out to safety. Then the prime minister gives him a medal or something."

"Not bad."

Tomas rolls towards me and rests his head on my chest like I'm his big pillow.

"So, where are we gonna *do it* tomorrow?" he asks with a whisper. "In here?"

"Maybe the river. I always thought it would be romantic there."

"*Romantic?*" Tomas teases.

"Yeah, like I'll go get some fruit. I'll pack a blanket and we'll make some sandwiches, take them in a cooler bag. I'll swipe one of Mum's bottles of wine she's just had sitting there in the cupboard for years. We'll take two glasses and have lunch down at the river, on the blanket."

"Like a picnic?"

"Yeah, a picnic."

"Sandwiches, mandarins, and nectarines for lunch?"

"Yeah. Then we'll have a glass of wine each. I'll lay you down while I kiss your neck."

"Stop it," Tomas says, pretending to bite my skin.

I giggle. "What do you think?"

"It sounds great," he says. "But you have to take it *slow*, this time."

I blush again, reminded of the embarrassment. I move past it and kiss his lips. Two kisses, then I rest back on my pillow. I'm still a little wet from the lake, but I'm too tired to care.

EIGHTEEN

I wake next to Tomas. He's beside me in my bed, still wearing his tank top and shorts. His mouth is open while he sleeps, just slightly. He's not snoring this time, though. He looks so peaceful, like he's dreaming about something nice. Maybe about me. I'm careful as I crawl off the bed. I don't want to wake him. I'll let him sleep for a little longer, while I ready myself for the day.

I find my towel on the floor and creep to the bathroom. In the shower, I take the soap and scrub myself harder than I've ever scrubbed before, because today's the day: *the day I'll become sure of everything.*

After the shower, I take my razor to my cheeks and notice that my black eye has darkened. It looks pretty sexy, if I'm being honest. I shave as close to the skin as I can, then wash it all away. I can't remember ever looking so fresh in the mirror. It brings a smile to my face.

I go back to my bedroom and Tomas is stirring on the bed. He moans and opens his eyes. "My head," he mutters. "I'm dying."

"You'll be right," I tease as I lean down and plant a kiss on his lips. I put on my white T-shirt and blue jean shorts. "Come down for breakfast."

Downstairs, all the kids are racing around. There's a headache growing inside me, edging at my temples. I pour two bowls of Coco Pops in the kitchen, then set one across from me at the table and pour the milk into mine.

Tomas stumbles down the stairs and arrives at the kitchen table, his hair in a mess, squinting through puffy eyelids. He adds milk to his bowl.

"So, where do we start with the plan for today?" he asks.

"You just stay here in bed. I'll come get you when I'm ready."

He nods and smiles, before eating another spoonful of Coco Pops. I go upstairs, grab my wallet and my phone. There's a message on my phone screen. I ignore it and squeeze everything into my pockets, because my body is rushing to get me out of the house. I head downstairs and Aunty Pam catches me at the bottom of the staircase.

"How's it going? You and Tomas getting along all right?" she asks.

"Yeah," I reply. "I wanted to ask you, would you mind if I borrowed your car for the day?"

"All day?" she asks.

I nod.

"Well, all right. I don't need it. Just put some petrol in it, eh?"

She hands me the keys to her station wagon. I dodge the kids and Mum, who's chasing them for a game, and head for the driveway.

I start Aunty Pam's car and it's hard to concentrate as

I reverse. I have flashes coming to my mind, images of all the things I want for today: everything I'll need to get, how it will all look when it's ready, how nervous I'll be when we're there together. How it will feel when it happens. How we'll do it again after a five-minute rest.

I start along the main street of the Mish. When I pass Tesha's house, Kalyn's truck is parked out front. I look for them as I pass, anger bubbling inside me for a moment. I thought it was all gone, but I guess not.

I drive into town, past the footy fields, which are now just bare and green. A woman throws a toy for her Labrador, which runs and jumps to catch it with its mouth. I pass the pub, and I don't see Ethan and the white boys on the balcony in the shade, nor in the beer garden.

I park behind the shopping center. It's a warm day with clear skies and I'm already starting to sweat. I walk inside and go to the bargain store. I search through the aisles and find a perfect brown handwoven picnic basket, which I buy for ten dollars. I go to the supermarket, rip plastic bags from their dispensers, and load them with nectarines and mandarins. I take a bunch of grapes and a bottle of cola for the drive home, and head for the checkouts. I wait by all the flowers in their bunches before the checkouts. Do boys get other boys flowers? Do boys like to receive flowers? I imagine that I would like to receive them, so I grab a bunch of yellow roses and take them with me to the checkout.

I walk it all to the car and drive back out. The street is busy as I wait at the traffic lights by the pub. I spot a parked police car in my rearview mirror and worry that Constable Rogers is going to walk by the car and see me. He'd probably strip me naked on the side of the road, or maybe he'd just shoot me. I don't have to find out, though, because the light turns green and I turn past the footy fields and head for the river.

I load everything into the picnic basket and walk along the pathway, through the bush to the river. The birds are singing at their loudest as I follow the bank along. The sun peeks through the treetops and the water flows strong against the rocks and fallen logs. I walk even farther.

It must take me an hour to get here, but I find the spot I'm looking for. It's a patch in the sand, under an ancient, giant willow tree, whose trunk has hollowed with age in places. The trunk is so thick, though, that it still has the strength to hold itself up. Grass grows through the sand in places, weak but determined. The patch itself is shaded by the willow tree's extended branches.

I realize I've forgotten to bring a blanket. I can just get one from home later, along with the wine and glasses. I hide the basket in some bushes by the willow tree and wipe the sweat from my brow. It's going to be perfect.

I start back for the station wagon, past the bushes and the dragonflies buzzing around. Then thunder rumbles above me. There are some gray clouds rolling in, and they aren't dawdling.

Just great.

I pull my phone from my pocket to check the weather forecast. Two messages on the screen catch my eye: an older one from Jarny and a newer one from Kalyn.

I open Jarny's message first.

You gay now?

I stop walking. My eyes leave the screen and a million things race through my mind. I read the message again. *You gay now?*

I open Kalyn's message.

I just saw Jarny . . . We should talk.

My heart feels like it's going to explode. They know? How? How do they know?

I text a reply to Jarny.

What you talking about?

I'm still standing at the river's edge. I don't want to move. I want to grow into one of the willow trees that hang around me. I want anything other than to be me right now. I take a deep breath and let it out again. My face feels hot, and I'm sweating like crazy.

My phone vibrates—a message from Jarny. I open it and it's a photo of me and Tomas, kissing at the lake last night. It's dark and it's blurry, the phone's camera clearly zoomed in as far as it can go, but it is definitely me and Tomas under the moonlight, kissing and holding each other in the water.

Another message comes from Jarny.

Troy saw you kissing him.

Tears come to my eyes. Their salt burns me. I start walking again, along the riverside. It's so hot around me as the bushes bash each other in the growing wind. I want to walk into them and get lost. Just disappear. Never come back. Jarny's shown the photo to Kalyn. That must be what his message was about. They both know. Everyone will know soon. There's no escape.

I wipe away my tears as I make it back to the station wagon. I open the driver's door and get in. Then I slam it shut and scream. I scream as loudly as I can for as long as I can, and then

I cry. I cry hard. I'm not sure of this yet. I'm not ready. I'm not ready to face this, and they know anyway. They hate me. They'll never talk to me again.

I start the car and head back to the Mish. I pass my place, check out Kalyn's, and his truck is parked out front. I don't want to look at it, though, so I do a U-turn, pull into my driveway. Inside, I pass all the screaming boys. Mum and Aunty Pam notice me but go back to their conversation at the kitchen table. I race up the stairs, push the bedroom door open, and find Tomas on his mattress, cross-legged. He looks up from his sketchbook, and his smile disappears after he's studied me for a moment.

"You all right?" he asks.

I take a breath and close the bedroom door. "We have to leave," I say. "I got Aunty Pam's keys. You have to leave with me now."

"Leave where?" he asks.

"Anywhere. Anywhere else." I cradle my face in my hands at the foot of my bed and the tears come again.

"What are you talking about?" Tomas crawls to me and rests his hands on my knees.

"They know. Jarny and Kalyn know. Troy sent Jarny a photo of us from the lake last night," I whisper, my voice breaking.

"Oh," he says.

"So we need to leave." I take his hands with mine. "Everyone will know soon. Then everything will change. Everyone will look at me different. They'll talk about us. They're probably talking about us now. We have to get out of here."

Tomas caresses my hands. "It's all right," he says.

"It's not all right!" I snap. "They know. They will all know.

I can't be *that* here, not on the Mish. No one will ever talk to me or look at me without feeling sick ever again."

"Jackson," he says, "I think you're overreacting. Just take a breath. All right?"

"Easy for you to say. It doesn't matter what they think of you. They aren't *your* family. They aren't *your* community."

"Jackson!" Tomas snaps now, taking hold of my wrist. "Just take a breath."

He breathes with me as I steady and breathe in and out, in and out, big deep breaths. He takes my hands again and holds them.

"It doesn't matter what they think of you," he says. "If they hate you for it, then why would you even want them in your life?"

"But," I begin, "everything will change now. We have to leave. I got Aunty Pam's keys."

"We can't just leave," Tomas interrupts. "I'm on bail. I'm fucked if I run away. And you've got a court date, so you'll be fucked too."

I start to calm down. My heart slows and my breathing returns to normal.

"They won't care," he continues. "And if they do, then fuck 'em."

I wipe away the tears on my cheeks. Maybe he's right.

"But this is the Mish," I say. "People like us . . . there's no one else like us here. We don't fit. I'm not ready for anyone else to know."

"I know," he whispers. He kisses the back of my hand. "I know, you're not ready. Neither am I. Just tell them that—that you're not ready. If they're really your mates, they will respect it. And they'll still love you. You're still you."

His hand is warm against my cheek as he caresses away my tears with his thumb.

"Am I still me? I'm not sure who I am."

"You are. You're fucking Jackson Barley. You'll always be Jackson Barley."

We sit there, silent. Tomas rest his forehead on mine and we breathe together. I realize the picnic is still just sitting somewhere in the bushes. The *perfect first time* will be washed away with the rain that's beginning to fall outside my window and drop onto the roof.

"You can just go talk to them," Tomas says. "They'll understand that you're not ready."

"You think?"

I look into his eyes. They are so brown and soothing.

"I can go with you, if you want?"

"It's okay. You stay here. I'm sorry. I'll go talk to Kalyn," I say.

"Good. Now stop being a drama queen."

Tomas reaches his mouth up to mine and kisses me. And maybe I'm not so wrong anymore, because it feels so right to be kissing his lips.

NINETEEN

The storm rolls over the Mish, growing more vicious with each passing second. I'm left stuck at my front door, ready to walk to Kalyn's, but with the rain bucketing down and the wind swirling like crazy. Mum and Aunty Pam have rushed their big canvas into the kitchen, where they're now struggling to dry some of the boys who were playing outside when the storm hit.

The clouds look black and purple in the sky. Lightning flashes in the distance and the thunder follows. All the boys start piling in front of the television, turning on the Xbox and scrambling for the controllers.

I walk back upstairs to my bedroom. I can hardly see the bush behind the house from my window because the rain is so heavy. I pull out my phone and reread the message from Kalyn: *I just saw Jarny . . . We should talk.*

I finally text a reply: *What Jarny say?*

I look back to Tomas, who smiles at me. He's working on his graphic novel, drawing square panels across the page, three boxes down, three boxes across. He writes the story onto the side of the page and leaves the three boxes beside each bit blank for illustrations.

My phone vibrates with a message from Kalyn.

He showed me the photo Troy sent him.

Another message comes. *I saw you and him on the canoe that day . . . After I dropped Jarny off, I wanted to double-check you didn't want a lift back . . . then I saw youse kissing . . . I was gonna wait until after Tommy left to talk to ya about it . . .*

I text back: *Might just be a phase. No big deal.*

He replies quickly. *You reckon?*

I stare down at Tomas. There was a time I did think that. But as I watch Tomas sit shirtless on his mattress, composing his graphic novel, I really don't think it is just a phase. I don't think there ever really was anything to figure out about myself.

I text back: *I dunno. I just don't want anyone to know.*

I move back to my bed and sit on its side. Another message comes from Kalyn: *I told him and Troy not to tell anyone, and I won't.*

The relief flowing over my body is like nothing I've ever felt. The tears are coming to my eyes again, and I wipe them away.

"You all right?" Tomas asks.

"Yeah. Kalyn's not gonna tell anyone."

Tomas nods and smiles at me, then goes back to his sketch-book. I look over the last message I sent.

I thought I wasn't ready, but maybe I am. Maybe Tomas has made me ready to accept this thing I've tried to stop being a part of who I am. Maybe.

I text back to Kalyn: *Thanks.*

I kick off my shoes and lie back on my mattress, listening to the rain beating down on our roof. I open my shirt to the breeze flowing through the window and close my eyes.

Kalyn sends me another text. *It's all right, brother.*

I look at the phone, and I'm suddenly feeling all right. Maybe it will actually all be okay. Maybe.

What was Jarny saying? I write.

Kalyn shoots back: *He's just a bit weirded out. Don't worry bout him.*

I turn my phone off and rest it on my stomach. The thunder booms louder, more violent. Through the rainfall, I hear Tomas's pencil hitting the page. I wonder where he gets the energy and the willpower from—the fire inside him—to focus on such a thing, after we've been exposed.

"What was juvie like?" I ask.

"It was all right," he says.

"Yeah? But how *was* it?"

"Boring," he says. "But it wasn't as scary as I thought it'd be. I had my own room and my own shower. We went to school and had programs in the afternoons."

"Programs? What kind of programs?"

"I dunno," he says, scribbling away. "People would come in from different places and talk to us about stuff, or we'd go to the pool, or have a game of footy."

"You had a pool?" I sit up and I know my eyebrows are nearly meeting my hairline.

"Yeah, just a little one."

"Did you have lots of fights with other kids?"

"Only had one fight, with this Leb kid. There are so many Kooris in there, though, so we sorta stuck together. The screws were the real assholes, always talking shit."

"The screws?"

"The workers. Most of 'em were cool, but a few talked a lot of shit." He looks up from his sketchbook. "I'm finished. Just needs pictures now."

I crawl off my bed and sit down opposite Tomas on his mattress. He flicks back through his pages to the start, and there's the cover page for the book. The title is spread across the paper in big block letters: THE BOY FROM THE MISH. It brings a smile to my face, warms me, knowing his hero is from here.

"I like the title," I say.

"Yeah? Well, it's an origin story, so I figure that saves me having to come up with a superhero name, like Superman or something. He's just a normal guy at the start."

I gaze upon the blank whiteness beneath the letters of the title. "So, what do you want for the cover pic?"

"Just him standing in front of the bush. And remember, black and muscly!"

I take the pencil and study the blank space for a moment. Then I sketch the hero's bare feet and place them on a grassy ground—I've decided he's standing with his back to us, facing the forest. I sketch his legs in torn, oversized pants; his ripped shirt, which hangs loose on his toned body. I give muscles to his forearms, a strong clench to his big, meaty hands. I hang his hair in a mess, which stretches down to his shoulder blades.

I give the trees spiky bundles for leaves and shade the trunks. I place them near and far, adding a depth to the picture, making the distance fuzzy, with our focus on the hero in the foreground.

"That's good," Tomas says as I show him the finished cover. The rain bangs on the roof like gun pellets and a big gust of wind swirls in through my window. The rain comes inside with it, and I rush to the window and close it while Tomas shields his sketchbook.

"Keen to start illustrating?" he asks. "I have the story here, and we can figure out how to turn it into panels."

He hands me the book and the pencil once more, and I flip past the cover page. His handwriting is pretty messy.

"Warren?" I giggle, realizing that's what he's named his superhero.

"Yeah, everyone knows a blackfella named Warren."

I start to read . . .

The people of the Mish were rattled. Two little girls had gone missing in the past fortnight. Word on the street was that they were playing in the bush. Now they were gone.

Warren, a boy from the Mish, was devastated to hear of their disappearances. He followed the news, watching every night as the police claimed they had no leads or evidence of anything. But Warren knew . . .

. . . Warren knew what lurked in the bush near the Mish. He knew of the evil and vicious creatures who'd terrorized residents of the Mish hundreds of years ago. He feared they might be back.

One month later . . . The government had declared a national tragedy. The police had searched the forests but found nothing except the shoe of one of the girls. Warren tried to calm the people of the Mish.

A town meeting was called at the Mish community hall. Uncle Raymond, a seasoned elder and warrior, declared there was only one solution: An Aboriginal person must travel into the bush, to find the missing girls.

Warren volunteered. His hand flew into the air, and he said he would be the one to do it. He knew of the danger that lurked in the bush, but he knew he must do what he had to for his people.

Warren departed his family home after a tearful farewell with his mother, little sister, and little brother. He took only a bag full of supplies and a hunting spear, passed down to him by his father.

He stood at the entrance of the bush and stared down the pathway. It was dark and gloomy, but Warren mustered the courage. He took a deep breath and ventured through.

He passed through the trees, through the swamps, through the bushes, over the footbridge across the river.

He ate dinner with the kangaroos. They shared salads and biscuits. Then he slept under the moon.

As he walked farther into the bush, Warren came across a den. It rested under the biggest tree he had ever seen.

Warren took his spear and crawled into the den. There was fur stuck to the walls, caught by the tree roots poking through the dirt. Warren crawled through . . .

. . . Warren reached the heart of the den. It looked like a cave, and there he saw the skeletons of the two missing girls.

As Warren cried, he heard footsteps behind him . . .

. . . Warren turned to see a big Hairy Man staring down at him. Its fur was thick and it was as tall as a mammoth. It looked down at Warren with its big red eyes.

Warren knew that this creature was a Doolagah. As he readied himself to spear it, he saw another Doolagah behind it, then another, then another!

Warren ran out of the den, but the Doolagahs chased him. He fought them in the forest, breaking his spear as he stabbed one of them. The others zeroed in on him and he hit them with a super-punch, which sent them all flying through the air.

More Doolagahs came out of the den. As Warren started to run from them, he realized he could fly. He flew through the air and back to the Mish.

Warren told the cops about the Doolagahs, and they told the government.

The government decided it would blow up the Mish in one hour, supposedly before the Doolagah infestation reached the other towns and villages.

The clock counted down at the Mish community hall. Warren raced to fight off the Doolagahs on the outskirts of town while the rest of the mob evacuated.

Warren fought the Doolagahs. He killed them one by one with his superhuman strength, but they kept coming and there were too many of them.

Warren ran back to the Mish. He saw the government helicopter in the sky, ready to drop its bomb.

He was about to fly away when he heard the cries of the children . . .

The children were stuck in their school. All the adults had left them. The doors were locked, but Warren ripped them open.

The alarm sounded from the Mish community hall. The countdown had reached zero. Warren saw the bomb begin to fall from the helicopter, just as the Doolagahs ran into the Mish.

Warren ripped off the wall of the school . . .

. . . His arms stretched like rubber and he grabbed all the children of the Mish . . .

. . . He flew them into the sky as the bomb landed on the street . . .

. . . The Mish exploded beneath him as he flew the kids past the helicopter . . .

. . . Past the clouds . . .

. . . Then Warren brought them down at the nearby village, where their parents and families were waiting for them.

All the people of the Mish gathered for Warren. They formed a parade and had a party.

The Prime Minister came to the parade. He offered Warren a medal, looping it onto his neck.

But Warren's greatest appreciation didn't come from the Prime Minister or the government. It came from the people who lived in his village, who praised him, their hero, "the Boy from the Mish."

"Damn," I say.

"You like it?" Tomas asks, eagerness on his face and light in his eyes.

"It's fucking amazing."

Tomas smiles and it is an amazing one, which stretches across his face as he blushes. It's the smile of a boy who doesn't get praised very often.

I take the pencil to the page and start to sketch his story from the descriptions.

"You really think it's good?" Tomas asks. I almost don't hear him over the rain on the roof.

"Yeah! I had no idea how good it would be," I say. "I think I underestimated you, Tommy."

I glance up from my page and there is a tear escaping Tomas's eye, though a half smile still rests on his face. He sniffles and the tears come streaming down.

"Hey," I whisper with a gentle voice. I put the sketchbook aside and shuffle closer to him on the mattress. "What's wrong?"

He looks to his lap, shakes his head. He takes a deep breath, and I feel like I'm about to cry with him.

"Nothin' I ever did was good," he says, with a shaky voice.

I wrap my arms around him. He falls against me and rests his head on my chest, crying for a few minutes before settling himself. Then he wipes away his tears and walks to the windowsill. I follow slowly behind him as he gazes into the gray and the thunder and the lightning and the rain.

The thunder still rumbles, but the rain sounds like it's falling lighter on the roof as Tomas opens the window.

"Are you all right?" I ask.

"Yep," he says. I lean against the windowsill beside him. "Where have you been this whole time?"

"I was right here," I say. A smirk comes to my face.

He wraps his arms around my body, shimmies in front of me, and rests his head against my chest, holding me against the windowsill. He presses his ear against my heart. I know he hears its fast beats, and that he'll be able to smell my deodorant and the excessive soap I used to scrub myself this morning. I wrap my arms around him too. I hope he feels safe in my arms.

The rain eases to gentle pitter-patters on the roof. The sun sets over the Mish, and Tomas snores on my bed. I'm still on the floor on his mattress, sketching his story. My wrist is sore as I finish the last image: the townspeople standing in two rows, clapping and cheering for their hero, Warren, the boy from the Mish.

I give the drawing a gentle blow to rid the page of lead dust, then I close the sketchbook and place it beside the mattress.

Tomas rolls over on my bed and moans, still asleep. He's dreaming, somewhere far away from here. His face shows he is relaxed and unworried.

I pick up my phone from the bedside table and turn it on, opening Kalyn's last message about Jarny. *He's just a bit weirded out. Don't worry bout him.*

But I do worry. I can't fucking help it. Maybe it's just part of my personality or my DNA or something—to worry forever about everything.

I text Kalyn a reply as I gaze outside to the easing rain: *Can I come talk?*

Kalyn texts back in a hurry: *Yeah, if you want.*

The feeling in my stomach is still there, even though he seems okay with knowing what he knows. The feeling just churns, squeezing somewhere inside me, like a knotted rope that feels the tightness of itself.

I pull on my shoes. I want to wake Tomas, so he knows where I'm going, but the peace I see on his face reassures me. As scared as I am to confront this, it's Kalyn. I've known him my whole life. He knows me better than anyone. He might have already guessed this, years ago.

Jarny, on the other hand, I'm not so sure about. He's never taken much seriously. I can already hear him making jokes about bum sex or something. He may actually hate me. But one thing at a time—off to Kalyn's.

TWENTY

The rain falls onto me as I step outside, though it's not too heavy anymore. I start along the main street of the Mish. My shoes splash in the puddles that have formed on the uneven road. I walk so slowly and let the rain wet me—whatever it takes to prolong my journey.

Up past the community center, I can see that Kalyn's pickup is still there, parked outside his house. My stomach twists at the sight of it. He's home. I want to turn back, join Tomas on my bed where it's safe, but my feet keep moving me forward.

The streetlight by the community center reflects off the water on the road. I step through its reflection as I pass. I arrive outside Kalyn's place, take a deep breath, step onto his lawn. It squishes like a sponge when I walk over it. I stop myself for another breath at the front door.

It's all right, I think.

It's Kalyn.

It'll be all right.

I knock on the door three times. I hear the radio inside, then footsteps. A figure appears through the glass pane. The door opens, and Kalyn stands there in a tank top and board shorts.

"Come in," he says.

I follow Kalyn inside to the kitchen. I'm relieved so far. The world hasn't ended just yet.

Kalyn opens a beer from the fridge. He offers me one but I shake my head, then I follow him into the backyard. He sits at the round glass table, shaded from the rain by the roof above us. He rubs his forehead and eyes, takes a big sip from his beer, and swallows a quarter of it in one gulp.

"So, do you want to talk about it?" he asks.

I don't want to speak. My throat has dried itself and I'm pretty much shaking like a jackhammer on gravel.

"Do we have to?" I ask as he takes another sip from his beer. "I mean, it's not a big deal . . . is it?"

"No," he says quickly. "Not a big deal." He looks at me and smiles, then looks to the rain gently falling onto the grass and dirt of his backyard. "We don't *have* to talk about it."

"We do though. Don't we?"

I study his face. I think he's blushing. It's hard to tell in the dark, but he probably feels the awkwardness I'm feeling, which has now replaced the fear in my stomach.

"I just want you to know . . . ," he says, cringing at his own words. "I just want you to know that I know. And it's okay. It's not a big deal, just like you said."

"Are you surprised?" I ask.

"I was," he says, taking another sip from his beer, "but then I wasn't. It sort of made sense, thinking about when we were little."

"How?" I look back to his gaze, which is veering off to the backyard.

"Like when we were little, you put on your mum's bra and told me to call you Jackie."

I burst into laughter, like it's been boiling inside me for years, just waiting for the perfect moment to escape. Kalyn laughs too.

"Shit, I forgot about that."

"It was funny as fuck," he says. "You put on her high heels and fell over and sprained your ankle. And I had to get you out of her stuff before I went to get help."

We laugh and laugh and laugh, and it's exhausting.

"But dressing up in Mum's clothes didn't mean anything. We were just playing. It didn't mean that I was . . . you know?"

"Yeah. I didn't think anything of it. I mean, did you know then?" Kalyn takes another sip from his beer.

"I knew I was different," I say.

"So . . . I mean, are you . . . you know . . . gay?" He struggles the words out of his mouth.

I dwell on the thought for a moment. *Gay.*

The word doesn't feel like what I am, if there is a word for what I am.

"I don't know. I'm still figuring that out, I guess."

Kalyn sits forward and looks at me again. Our eyes meet and he's forcing back a smile.

"Well, whenever you figure it out, don't worry about anything. You're my cousin. I don't care if you like different things. What matters is we're here for each other, like we've always been."

Kalyn takes another sip from his beer and finishes it. He goes inside to get another, and I let the smile come to my face while he's gone. I could cry from the relief and the happiness he has given me with those words. I don't want him to see me cry, though, so I quickly wipe away an escaping tear.

Kalyn returns through the sliding door and places a beer in front of me. I twist off the lid and it is so cold when I pour it down my throat.

"Does Jarny hate me?" I ask.

"I dunno," Kalyn says. "Jarny's just *Jarny*. He'll get over it."

"What if he doesn't?"

Kalyn takes a sip from his beer. "If he doesn't, then fuck him."

"I just don't want to lose anyone," I say. "I'm not ready for people to know anything."

"I know," he says. "He'll get over it."

A light bulb lights itself and explodes inside my head.

"Wait," I begin, sitting forward. "Did you ask me if you could go for Tesha because you saw me kiss Tomas on the canoe?"

"Yeah," he says. "I figured you'd be okay with it."

"Jesus." I chuckle. "I mean, I still like girls, I think."

"Really?" Kalyn looks at me with those puppy-dog eyes.

"I think I might. I dunno."

Kalyn takes another sip. "I won't keep seeing her if you don't want me to."

"No," I say, almost giggling. "No, it's fine. I could never go all the way with her anyway."

"Oh, I know," Kalyn says. We both laugh a nervous kind of laughter, and I worry he now knows the size of my flaccid penis. I take a sip of beer and let it relax me.

"What if Jarny tells everyone?" I ask. "What if Troy keeps sending the photo around?"

"Jarny won't. Troy won't," Kalyn is quick to reply. "I told them not to, so they won't."

"You sure?" I look to his eyes.

He thinks for a moment, taking a sip from his beer. "Well, if they do, we'll just have to kill 'em."

We both laugh again. We finish our beers, then move on to another one each.

"You should come back to school next term," Kalyn says. "It's just one more year to go."

"School? I can't be at that school, being Aboriginal *and* gay!"

"Well, you don't have to tell anyone. And besides, things are a lot better these days for the LGT . . . B . . . people . . . I'll be there, anyway. If it does turn into a problem, they'll have to go through me first."

I sip my new beer and shake my head. "I'll think about it. I just don't think I can do another year."

"How am I meant to survive geography alone with all the white people?"

We laugh again.

"Yeah. I guess if you need me to *carry you* to graduation, I'll think about it." I take another sip. "And I think it's LGBTQ . . . fuck. I know there are more letters!"

We sit there for hours, drinking and talking, then I stagger home. The thunder rumbles and the rain starts bucketing down again, heavy and freezing.

I burst through the front door of my house. The water drips from my body and splashes onto the floor. Aunty Pam wakes on the couch when I close the door. I give her a nod as I pull off my shoes and socks. I stumble up the stairs and into the shower. The water streams down over me, so hot, and I feel it wash away all the panic and the worry, because Kalyn's okay with me.

I dry myself and stumble to my bedroom. Tomas is sitting on his mattress. I close the door and see he is examining the pictures I've drawn into the panels he's marked in his sketchbook. He looks up to see me as I stumble across to my dresser.

"These are so good," he says.

"Yeah?"

"The drawings are perfect. They're almost exactly what I imagined."

"*Almost?*" I say, dragging out the word as I gently tackle him on his mattress.

He slides the sketchbook to the floor and positions himself to let me lie on top of him. I kiss him and he kisses me back.

"Have you been drinking?" he asks.

"Yes."

"Where was my invite?"

"You were snoring your brains out," I say, teasing him.

"So just wake me up." He gives me a playful jab in the stomach.

I start to laugh, and he pushes me back. He forces me onto the mattress and kisses me again. It's a deep kiss, and I let him in. I've never wanted to stay stuck inside a kiss so badly. He grabs my wrists and pins them over my head. His lips smack as he takes them away from mine. He catches his breath on top of me and releases my wrists.

"Aunty Pam said we're leaving in two days," he says.

"Two days?" I rest my hands on his waist. Sadness returns to my stomach in a flash.

"Yeah. I'm sorry we couldn't go on your *perfect date*." His face has fallen. He looks like he's about to cry.

"Hey, we can still go on that date. I want it to be with you."

"The storm's meant to last until at least tomorrow, though."

"That's all right," I snap, though it's not all right. "Next time, then. You can come visit, after the judge sees your work and decides you'll be fine. Or I'll come visit you. It's only a fifty-dollar bus ticket."

"You sure?"

"Yeah. It'll be okay."

"What if you forget me? Like all the caseworkers and foster families? What if you find someone better?" A tear escapes his eyelids and rolls down his cheek.

"I won't," I promise. I've never been surer of anything, though I'm not as sure that he won't forget me.

We shift our bodies and I rest my head on Tomas's chest. I feel embarrassed about my plan. *My perfect plan.* Now the basket is soaked at the river. The skins of the nectarines have probably washed away. Maybe the river fattened and ate the whole basket. But fuck it. I can't just give up without trying. I still want that perfect first time. I want it with Tomas, and I want it now. Why should the rain stop us?

"I still want that date," I whisper. "Remember when I told you about how the Land Council would do that walk up the mountain? Wanna go tomorrow? No one ever goes up there anymore. Screw the rain."

"Up the mountain? Yeah, okay. Tomorrow."

TWENTY-ONE

The clouds are looming large and gray in the sky when I wake. The morning sun can hardly break through. The silence is amazing, though. There's no more rain bashing down on the roof, no thunder roaring above.

"It's gonna storm," Aunty Pam says downstairs during breakfast, interrupting me and Tomas talking about the walk we're about to take up the mountain.

"So we'll take an umbrella," I say.

"Yeah," Tomas says, backing me up. "We'll just take an umbrella."

Aunty Pam sighs. "And rain jackets."

"It's, like, a hundred degrees," I protest.

"It's a long way up there," Aunty Pam says, looking at me with her wisdom eyes. "Long enough to get sick in the rain."

I roll my eyes, and Tomas forces back a laugh.

Mum and Aunty Pam load all the kids' clothes into the washing machine and put the washed clothes into the dryer. I sneak a bottle of wine into my backpack and take two fancy wineglasses from the cupboard.

I rummage through my dresser to find my rain jacket. Then Tomas takes Mum's umbrella and we head out the front door. The bottle and the glasses rattle in my backpack, so I take off the jacket and wrap the glasses in it. We walk along the main street of the Mish in our tank tops and short-shorts, flip-flops on our feet. The clouds still roll across the sky. They grow darker every minute.

We pass Kalyn's place, head downhill. Then I take Tomas through the bush, onto the pathway to the mountain. The pathway isn't flawless, just a scattering of wooden planks on the ground, which act as stepping-stones. They weave through the bushes and trees, which cover us in darkness as we walk.

My legs are burning as I lead Tomas up the incline. It grows steeper and steeper, and the dirt and fallen twigs crackle beneath our feet. The brightness of the gray sky comes through as we trek higher. Birds sing in the trees around us, as do the insects. The mosquitoes bite at my ankles, but I just swipe them away.

We arrive at the wooden stairs, which are really just planks stuck in the ground. I climb first and Tomas follows. The steps wiggle beneath our feet. I tread carefully; there are no railings to hold on to.

Rocks stick out from the mountain. I know they probably extend deep under the surface. We climb past the tree line and higher still. Tomas stops to turn around, and the tops of the trees surrounding the Mish look like a green, hazy sheet. He stares for a moment, so I wait.

"It's so pretty," he says. Then he roars out across the view, and it echoes over the trees and bounces from the neighboring mountains in the far distance. He turns back to me with a smile and then roars to the landscape again, as if he's replying to his own echoed roar.

"Jeez. If you like this, just wait till you get to the top," I say.

I continue climbing and Tomas picks up his speed, passing me and leaping from step to step.

"Careful!"

He doesn't listen. He jumps his way up the mountain, and I watch the steps wiggle under his weight. But he doesn't care. It makes me smile to see him having so much fun. He howls ahead of me, like a wolf looking for a mate. I howl back and he laughs. And fuck it. I start to leap too, jumping from step to step.

I try to catch up to him, but he's disappeared past some bushes that hang over the path. When I duck underneath them, I see Tomas resting on the steps ahead, with his hands on the back of his head.

"Hurry up!" he shouts, and it echoes into the atmosphere. A raindrop lands on my face, right on my black eye.

We reach the end of the stairs, which peter out onto a flat surface covered in dirt and fallen leaves, less than twenty meters from the very top. This is as far as we can go; it's too steep from here. The trees on the peak above hang over us, their green leaves rich with color.

A metal fence has been put up around the edge. Tomas stands there with his hands on the railing. I catch my breath and join him as he looks out over the distance. The houses of the Mish on the ground look no bigger than blocks of Lego. Tomas walks to the other side of the lookout, leans against that railing, and again I follow him. We can make out the cars traveling through the main street of town below, and the specks of bodies on the beach. The drop below us is so definite: a straight fall into the trees below.

"You know," I say, "we could just jump. Then we won't have to go to court and we won't have to face anyone. You won't have to go back to Sydney."

Tomas looks to me with a smirk on his face. "We wouldn't be able to have your perfect date then, would we?" he teases.

Another raindrop falls onto my head. Then another, and another, and then it's bucketing down. Tomas laughs as we run to the cover of the arching mountain peak hanging over the lookout. My hair is all wet and so is his. I have to catch my breath again.

I release the backpack from my back and pull out the bottle of wine. Tomas sits on the dirt with me while I pull out my rain jacket and unwrap the wineglasses.

I pour the wine into our glasses and hand his to him. He holds it with both hands.

"Cheers," I say. We clang our glasses together and each take a sip.

"This is fucking disgusting," Tomas says, screwing his face into a fold of wrinkles.

I just chuckle, rest my hands back on the dirt, and feel the stress in my muscles fade away. "I'm sorry there aren't any nectarines or mandarins, or a picnic blanket . . ."

"Or a picnic *basket*," Tomas interrupts.

He takes another sip from his glass, clearly forcing the wine down his throat. I do the same. We finish off our drinks as the rain beats down on the dirt. The wind sprays the rain into us for a moment, then goes away again.

"So . . . we just have sex now?" Tomas asks.

Nervousness begins to churn in my stomach again. My throat dries and my heart starts to race.

"Um," I cough, "yeah. I mean, if you want to."

I stare at Tomas as he nods. He doesn't really look at me or speak or wear any expression on his face. He's just blank and quiet, staring at some point in the middle distance. I spot his pulse on his neck and realize his heart is racing as fast as mine, if not faster. I place my hand on his thigh, slow my breathing. He looks down at my hand, then he places his hand on top of mine and holds it. His palm is sweaty.

I shuffle myself across the dirt, closer to him. I aim my lips for his and we kiss. I can't help but hear the rain falling around us, feel its drops splashing from the dirt up to our bodies.

Tomas kisses me fast. I slow him down, and his lips are so soft on mine. I reach for his tank top. I pull it over his head, and I hate that moment we have to stop kissing while I get it off. We kiss again and he grasps my top. He takes it from my body and drops it on the dirt.

My arms tremble as I crawl on top of Tomas. He lies back, and I position my waist between his legs. I rest into him as I kiss his chest.

"Fuck," he says.

I stop kissing. "What's wrong?"

"This dirt is fucking rough," he says. "It's stabbing my back."

I move my hand behind his head and pull him up. We switch positions and I lie on my back. But he's right. This dirt is fucking rough as hell. The tiny rocks are jabbing me, and it feels like my skin is peeling as we kiss and move our bodies against each other.

"Maybe if we stand up," I say.

Tomas sighs and pulls me to my feet. We continue kissing, standing there under the rock. The sharpness of his facial hair grazes against my skin, and the warmth of our bodies combines as we hold each other so tight.

I reach for the waist of Tomas's shorts, but as I tuck my fingers inside, I have to stop myself. I stop kissing him and take my hands away.

"I'm sorry. I can't do this standing up. It's not . . ."

"Perfect?" Tomas interrupts.

I just nod. "I'm sorry."

Tomas smiles and hugs me. He gives me a kiss on the shoulder and rests his chin there.

"There's still time to take Aunty Pam's car," I whisper. "We can still run away."

Tomas chuckles. He slips his hands into my shorts and takes me. I do the same as we stand there. The wind brings the rain onto us again, a spray landing on my neck, but I don't care. My forehead rests against his as we breathe together. It's just us on this mountain—me and Tomas.

When we're done, we just hold each other, and I realize how it feels: It feels perfect.

"You know what? I . . . I don't really think I'm *ready*," he says.

"You're not?"

He shakes his head, and he honestly looks like he's about to break down and cry.

"Why didn't you tell me?" I ask.

"You had this perfect plan," he says. "And I know you wanted to do it before I leave. I didn't want to ruin it, but I'm just not really ready. I'm sorry."

"Don't be silly." I smile, planting a kiss on his lips.

He holds me again, and I just want to stand in his arms at the top of the mountain forever, as the rain falls around us and traps us here.

We don't even bother to drink any more of the shitty wine. As soon as the rain eases, we start back down the stairs. Their wooden boards are slippery in the wet, so we go slowly. The rain comes again, and we climb off the stairs and crawl backwards down the dirt and leaves that cover the mountain, continuing beside the steps that way until we reach the pathway at the bottom, which has turned to mud. The backpack has gotten heavier on my back, and I worry the rain has gotten in there.

"Great idea bringing me up here," Tomas teases. He unleashes the umbrella as we walk along the pathway through the bush. I huddle close to him under its cover. The thunder roars and lightning strikes from the clouds. "And now we're gonna die by lightning!"

I just laugh as we power walk through the bush. We make it back to the road and start for home.

"Next time, I choose where we go," Tomas says. I laugh at him again as he examines his mud-covered feet and flip-flops.

Back in the Mish, I notice Owen's car is parked in front of Kalyn's truck. As we approach, Owen and Jarny make a run for it from Kalyn's front door to the car. Jarny spots us and stops in the rain.

I almost halt in my tracks, but Tomas keeps me walking. Jarny keeps his stare on us as we pass.

"I thought we were brothers," he shouts. The rain is loud as it hits the umbrella and the road. It's hard to make out his words clearly.

I stop and turn to him. "What?"

"I said *I thought we were brothers*. Why didn't you ever tell me you're a poofter?"

He stands there, staring and judging. I can hardly make out his face in the rain, but I know he isn't smiling. Owen stands beside the car, and I know he's hearing all of this as he stares at me too.

"What did you call me?" I ask, knowing full well what he called me. I step out from under the umbrella.

"A *poofter*," Jarny says, cutting through my whole body with the word. "That's what you are, right? A poofter? Or do you prefer *faggot*? Or maybe just *homo*?"

I'm not a person anymore. I'm just a ball of fire, of raging lava. I'm a flaming comet of rage, moving towards Jarny. Owen races to stop me, but I land a punch on Jarny's cheek. He falls back against the car with a bang. He slides down and collapses onto the road, where the rain pounds down on him.

Owen steps in front of me and pushes me back. I puff out my chest as I take my eyes from Jarny to Owen. I'm ready to punch him too.

"Walk away," Owen says.

I stand tall, still as a rock, my whole body filled with anger and hate and absolute adrenaline.

"Walk away," he repeats. Another shove against my chest.

I look back down to Jarny. His arm flails as his hand tries to find his face. I see the red growing on his cheek as the rain hits him. I look back to Owen and see his eyes. They're not filled with hate; they are sad and worried and just wanting me to leave. Kalyn's front door slams. I see him racing from the lawn into the rain.

I turn away, walk back to Tomas, whose fists are clenched at his sides. I take his hand and we walk on along the main street of the Mish. His fist releases its clench in my palm, then he guides his fingers between mine. My other hand is starting to burn. There's an aching rock hardening under the skin, against the bones. I bring it up to my eyes. It's wet and red and purple, and growing bigger by the second.

TWENTY-TWO

Tomas drops the umbrella to the grass, and I burst through the front door of my house, still holding his hand, dragging him behind me. The boys all turn to look at us from the couch and mattresses. I lead Tomas up the stairs and into my bedroom.

I sit at the foot of my bed with Tomas, and the pain suddenly explodes in my hand. Tomas takes it and holds it with both of his, examining it. Amid all the red and purple, there's a cut on my central knuckle, spilling a small amount of blood.

"Might be broken," Tomas says.

His hair is all wet. So is mine. I feel the water trailing from my forehead. I look at his face, the damp mop of hair draping over his ears and forehead and the back of his neck.

"You're beautiful," I whisper.

The smell of roasting chicken has made its way upstairs, and darkness is falling outside my window. Tomas follows me across the hallway to the bathroom, and I run cold water over my swollen hand.

"I reckon you should probably go to the hospital," Tomas says.

"Nah. I'll deal with it after you leave tomorrow," I say.

Back in my bedroom, I realize there is dried mud and dirt all over my carpet. Our feet and legs are still dirty.

I picture Jarny—the image of him on the road as the rain fell on him, his arm flailing about. I worry I might have killed him.

Maybe he's just confused and angry. Maybe he hates himself, for not being approachable enough for me to be able to tell him before now. Maybe he just doesn't want to lose me, thinking I'll change and move to the city and hang out with all my gay friends and go to gay nightclubs and pierce my ears and tattoo a rainbow on my wrist. Maybe he thinks I'll start talking gay and acting gay and that I won't be the same person he's known all these years. And maybe I will change. Maybe just a little bit. Maybe that would be okay.

I take my towel to the shower, let the hot water fall over me, and just stand there. When I come back, Tomas rolls over on his mattress to look up at me, and I drop my towel and reach my good hand down to him. He takes it and I lift him from the floor. I flick off the bedroom light with my bad hand, and the act stings it like fire.

Under the moonlight, we crawl onto my bed. Tomas places his pillow next to mine. I kiss him for so long, then we stare into each other's eyes. It's dark, but I can see his eyes glistening. We don't speak, only stare, and I try not to blink. I pull the blanket over us. I tuck my arm under his head, and he rests his head on my chest. I hold him and feel him warm against me. I think he's listening to my heartbeat. I can feel it beating under his ear, and it's slow. I am so calm with him now. It's the best feeling in the world.

*   *   *

I don't want to open my eyes as the morning sun falls over us. I do, though, and I gaze upon Tomas's sleeping face and listen to his slow breathing, to the snores threatening to become louder. Sadness comes to my stomach again as I watch him sleep with his head on the pillow beside mine.

I move my thumb to his cheek and brush his skin. I'm gentle, because I don't want to wake him. He's beautiful when he dreams. Maybe he's dreaming of another life—one where we aren't separated, where we can spend every second staring into each other's eyes and kissing and holding each other, and where we're both ready to have sex and that's all we do all night, every night.

"Breakfast!" Mum shouts up the stairs.

Tomas wakes at the sound of her voice. He opens his eyes slowly, like a newborn kitten forcing its eyelids open to the light. It's not long before he wears on his face the same sadness I am feeling, because today is the day he leaves.

He sits up and dangles his legs over the edge of the bed. I crawl to meet him there. I place my feet on the floor beside his and plant a kiss on his bare shoulder, and he turns to me with a small smile. I smile back.

"How's your hand?" Tomas asks.

"It's fine," I say, but it's not. It's burning and I can hardly move my fingers. But that doesn't matter to me right now—all that matters is that Tomas is leaving today. "I can always call you at Aunty Pam's house. And she has my number, so you can call anytime."

Tomas just gives me that same smile, which shows sadness

but also relief. Maybe I'm relieved too, because once he's gone I won't have to sneak around anymore or feel like everyone is watching us.

Tomas stands from the bed and puts on his shirt and football shorts from the floor. I get dressed into a tank top and a pair of boxers.

We meet at the bedroom door. We stand still there, gazing into each other's eyes. I take his hand, hold it for a moment, then pull him against me. I kiss him and he kisses me back. The sadness has awoken again in my stomach, climbing its way to my throat. But Tomas's warmth is stronger—his care, his kindness, his compassion, which he gives to me through his lips. He wraps his arms around me and holds me tight.

When he pulls his lips away we stay there holding each other, and I run my fingers over his cheek, through his hair. I want to savor every strength he gives me, as he tightens his grip. I want to savor the smell of his skin, the feeling of the sharp hairs of his chin as he rests it on my shoulder, the feeling of his heart beating against my body.

I kiss him again. I want to savor the taste of his lips, his tongue. A tear rolls down his cheek. I wipe it away with my thumb, take his hand, and rest it against my cheek. I want to savor the feeling of his fingers on my face, his gentle touch, the warmth of his palm.

Let us stay here holding each other for as long as it takes to be ready to walk out that door.

I release Tomas and we rest our foreheads together. Our noses brush. I reach for the doorknob and plant my hand on it. I take a breath, then open the door.

We walk downstairs and are greeted by eggs, sausages, and bacon. All the kids are spread around the table. We join them and eat, and it's the best meal I've ever tasted. The kids throw their food at each other. Me and Tomas join in, and Mum and Aunty Pam yell at all of us, but we just laugh.

After breakfast, Mum and Aunty Pam gather everyone in the backyard. I put on a hoodie and pull the sleeve down over my swollen hand.

"We finally finished," Aunty Pam says.

Resting on the grass is their big canvas painting. It's at least three meters long and it stretches wide, from the back shed to the clothesline. They've glued smaller square canvases together at their edges to make this big thing. The colors catch me first: a dark blue overall, with red circles and symbols, interlaced with black symbols and yellow dots. It is quite magical to look at. I thought that I'd seen it before, but now that it's done, it might as well be a whole new painting that they've put together.

"The river flows through the middle," Mum says, kneeling down and hovering her hand over the wavy white lines, like she's surfing her hand in the wind outside a car window. Their river is white and blue, and its waves flow from one side of the artwork to the other. On one side of the flowing river are painted black outlines of bodies, each with two white eyes.

"These are the mothers," Mum says, then she moves her guiding hand from their bodies to the other side of the river, where there are smaller painted black figures, which almost resemble peanuts. They each have two smaller white eyes. "And these are the children."

At the very center of the painting is a series of circles within circles, with yellow lines branching out and fading into either side of the river. If I got on my knees and looked closer, I'm sure I would see these lines reaching to each of the mothers and each of the children.

"This is the culture that reaches out to them, connects them, so that they might find each other again one day," Mum says, pointing at the circles.

"It's beautiful, Aunt," Tomas says.

And it really is beautiful. Mum has been really surprising recently. I knew she was an artist, but this is more than just a work or a project. This is feeling. This is spirit. This is something deeper, something that is hard to visualize until you see it right in front of you and let it sink inside you.

I gaze over the footprints, the kangaroo tracks, all painted in black on the background. They are almost hidden in the dark blue.

Aunty Pam stops behind Mum, whose fingernails are still stained with paint. Mum stands up and gazes over her master-piece, her hard work. I feel I have never been prouder to be her son. I want to go and hug her for the longest time. But I won't. I'll just stand here and admire what she and Aunty Pam have done.

"Where you gonna put it?" I ask.

"I reckon we'll put it up in the lounge room. It should cover the whole side wall."

We head back inside. I help Mum plant the painting on hooks in the lounge room. It's almost a perfect fit, and I realize it's actually slightly smaller than I'd thought it was, once I see it up there on the wall.

Tomas and all the kids take turns showering and get dressed. The bags are all packed, and Aunty Pam orders me to help her load the luggage into the back of the station wagon while Tomas gets his stuff from my bedroom.

Mum shares a hug and a laugh with Aunty Pam as all the kids exchange hugs with Henry. Then they all climb into their seats and fasten their seat belts. Tears roll down Henry's cheeks, and he complains that he wants his cousins to stay longer.

"Me too, bro," I say as I rub his shoulder. "Me too."

"Where's Tomas?" Aunty Pam asks.

I walk back inside and stop at the bottom of the staircase. Tomas is there, standing at the top of the stairs with his bags in hand. Our eyes meet. We know this is it. I just keep reminding myself that he will only be a phone call away. Tomas takes a breath, then starts a slow walk down the stairs, and I lead him out the front, where he loads his bags into the back of the station wagon, squeezing them past the blankets and pillows, and closes the door.

Tomas gives Mum a kiss on the cheek and thanks her for having him, then walks back to me as Aunty Pam climbs into the driver's seat. I can see in his eyes that he wants to hold me, kiss me again. I want the same. I want to kiss those lips and hold him tight, dig my fingers into his back and trap him here. Instead, I offer him a handshake with my good hand. His grip is tight as he shakes it back, and I hold his hand tightly as well. We release our grip and just hold our palms against each other for a moment. He's so warm.

"I'll call you soon," he says. "Or you can call me."

I just nod and smile. "Happy New Year," I mutter with a breaking voice.

Aunty Pam starts the car as Tomas climbs into the passenger

seat beside her. He fastens his seat belt and looks to me through the window, and I walk across the lawn and follow the car as Aunty Pam reverses. Henry follows me. We stop at the front gate, and Tomas offers me a wave as they sit still there for a moment. I wave back and smile, then Aunty Pam puts the car into drive.

I watch the station wagon as it travels along the main street of the Mish and disappears around the corner. The tears threaten to come, and my legs begin to shake at the knees, but I just take a deep breath. In and out.

Back inside, I vacuum the floor in the lounge room while Mum shoves all the mattresses back into storage. My hand aches, but I let it ache. I think about the pain, focus on it—the staleness of my bones and the fire that burns around it.

Henry cries for a bit, but then he settles, and he and Mum start a kids' movie on the couch together. I go upstairs to my room and close the door. Tomas's mattress is still on the floor. I fall onto the sheets and the pillow. It all still smells like him. I close my eyes. I could use a good sleep.

"Jackson!" I hear Mum shout.

I open my bedroom door and peek my head out. "What?" My voice croaks.

"You got visitors."

I drag myself up and see Kalyn coming up the stairs, treading slowly. Then I see Jarny behind him. Jarny glances at me, then back to his feet. His cheek is swollen and black. My heart begins to race at the sight of him, and the anger comes back to my stomach as I hear him again saying: *poofter.* I hear all the words he could have called me.

"What's he doin' 'ere?" I ask.

"Let us come in," Kalyn says. "Jarny wants to talk to ya."

I'm tempted to just shut the door in Kalyn's face, but I step back and walk to my window. The door closes, and I turn around to see them both standing at the foot of my bed. I lean back against the windowsill, and Kalyn takes a few steps closer to me.

"Did everyone leave? Tommy too?" he asks.

"Left today."

"Right. Well, we just wanted to come see ya. Jarny has something he wants to say."

"I'm sorry," Jarny says. He walks around and sits on the side of my bed. "I don't know why I'm such a prick. I was just . . . angry . . ."

"Angry about what?" I ask. I'm frowning with such effort as I try to understand him.

"I don't know. Because you never told us. I thought I had a right to know that. And because of Tomas. It was like he just came in and changed you." Jarny keeps his eyes on his shoes, hood over his head.

"What are you talking about?"

"Like, you were this whole other person. I was angry you were gone. And then I was angry because I know he didn't just *change* you—it was that you couldn't be yourself . . . because of us. But I'm not angry anymore, because I'm just sorry. I'm sorry for what I said. I know now it isn't my *right* to know these things, not unless you want me to."

"I'm not gone. I'm still me."

"But you're gay now."

"I didn't just *turn gay*." I'm almost laughing. "I don't even

210

know if *gay* is the right word for me, but whatever it is, I'm still me. It's not a big deal."

"I didn't mean that . . . It's just the Mish, though," Jarny says, finally looking at me. "There're people here who'll say worse shit to you than I did."

"I know. I'm still figuring it out, you know? I always thought it was just a phase. But it's not."

Kalyn clears his throat louder than anyone has ever cleared their throat before.

"I think what Jarny is really trying to say is that we don't care if you're not straight, or if you like boys or whatever, because we love you. You're our brother. It'll be a bit tough here, probably. But *we'll* be here. And if anyone says any stupid shit to you, they'll have to deal with us as well. Right, Jarny?"

"Yes. Exactly," Jarny says, nodding his head.

"Thanks," I say. I can hardly believe we are having this conversation. "You know, if shit does go down," I say, "or someone says something about me, you don't have to defend me or anything."

"Of course we do," Kalyn says. "We will."

"Yeah," Jarny says, nodding.

A smile comes to my face like it was struck on there by lightning. The smile brings the tears with it, and Kalyn and Jarny both hug me.

"I deleted the photo," Jarny says. "Kalyn watched me delete it, and we made Troy delete it too."

"Good. Sorry about your face," I say to Jarny.

"Sorry 'bout your hand," Jarny replies.

I look at it, still swollen and red and purple. "Should probably get it checked out, eh?"

Jarny rolls himself a cigarette. He offers me one, but I decline. He only smokes half of it, out my window, then we all go for a walk. We walk along the main street of the Mish, past Kalyn's house and then down the narrow track around the mountain. We pass the farmland and cross the bridge over the river and into town.

We arrive at the medical center. Kalyn and Jarny sit with me while we wait for forty minutes on the seats by the reception desk. The doctor calls me in and inspects my hand. After an X-ray, he tells me I've broken the "metacarpal neck" and calls it a *boxer's fracture*. He places a cast on my hand, which goes up to my wrist.

I go with Jarny and Kalyn for a feed of fish and chips, then we head back to the Mish. Kalyn invites me to come in and have a beer with him and Jarny at his place. I decline, but as I watch them walk into the yard, I feel an overwhelming gratitude for them. I couldn't explain it to them if I tried.

At home, Mum and Henry are still on the couch, watching a different movie. I go back upstairs into my bedroom, close the door, and once again plant myself on Tomas's mattress. I don't want to get up from it—not while it still smells like him.

TWENTY-THREE

It's been two weeks since Tomas left, and it must be the hottest day all summer. There are two fans blowing in the kitchen and two in the lounge room, but they just puff the hot air through the house.

"I wanna go back to school," I say as I enter the kitchen.

I've shocked Mum, who's pulling a wet tea towel from the freezer. "You wanna go back now?" she asks with wide eyes as she drapes the towel over the back of her neck. She's even more shocked than when she found out my hand was broken.

"Yeah. It's just one more year. And it'd be good to have my diploma as well."

"What's changed your mind?"

"Just feeling good about it, I guess," I say.

"Well, all right. I'll give the school a call when the teachers go back next week."

I give Mum a kiss on the cheek, then head out the front to meet Kalyn and Jarny, who are waiting for me in Kalyn's pickup. We pass some campervans and cars towing trailers as we drive down the mountain and turn into the camping ground. Most of the campers have left, heading back to their own towns and their own lives, leaving us behind until next summer. Troy's camp is still here, though, and he's standing at his fairy lights as we pass.

"Come round tonight," he calls as we slow down. "We're headin' home tomorrow!"

"After the men's group, brother!" Jarny shouts back to him.

We drive along the dirt tracks and follow the road into the bush, ending our drive at the fence by the lake. Unloading the canoes from the back of the track, we carry them to the water. Jarny gets in one of the canoes while I share with Kalyn, and we paddle across the lake to where the men are gathering at our spot on the bank.

I step into the shallow water and Kalyn pulls the canoe onto the sand. The sausages are cooking over the little bonfire and their smoky delight fills the air. Finding my painting behind its rock, I take it to paint beside Kalyn and Jarny, and we are silent. I bring the brush to the brown paint on the cardboard and add some more dots to my turtle's shell.

Uncle Charlie arrives with his grandson, Will, who works at the community center. Uncle Charlie calls us all over to the bank, and we each make a sausage sandwich and sit on the sand. In a circle, we introduce ourselves and speak about what we want to get from the men's group this year.

When it comes to me, I say, "I just want to stay connected. Sometimes I feel like I don't belong here, but I need to stay connected to my mob."

Uncle Charlie tells us a story about this rooster he owned when he was a boy. He speaks about how his rooster was always horny and tried to have sex with the other chickens, like a dog in heat. We just laugh, mostly at the way he tells his stories. Usually they have morals, but I think this time he just wants to have a laugh.

After the chat, some of the men and boys go back to painting. Some go for a swim in the lake. Some throw a line in and fish. I just stand in the shallow water and bring a handful of water over my head. I listen to the birds who speak in the trees. I listen to their sounds as they flutter from branch to branch and fly away. I listen to the sound of the water against my legs and feel its coolness in the summer heat.

"Jackson," Uncle Charlie says, finishing up his sausage sandwich. "Come for a walk with me, son."

I follow after him, dripping water, wearing just my football shorts. We walk along a little pathway through the bush, and I slow my pace to Uncle Charlie's after I catch up.

"Where's Uncle Rex today?" I ask.

"Oh, he was feeling a bit sick today," Uncle Charlie says. "He'll be right, though."

We come out of the bush onto another bank. We are alone, and I don't hear the men or boys from the group, or the campers up the lake.

"I heard you had a fight with Jarny," Uncle Charlie says.

"Not a fight, just a punch, really."

"Did he do something to you?" he asks, turning to see me. His eyes are brown and dark, surrounded by the dark brown of his skin.

"No, I was just angry because of something he said. But we're all good now."

"Usually, when we call someone something, like what he called you, it's because we don't understand. And when we don't understand, we get scared. So we try to make things normal again and we attack what's making us scared. It just makes things worse."

He takes a seat on a flat rock overlooking the lake.

"So you know what he called me then?" I ask.

He points to the ground beside him. The anxious feeling is returning to my stomach as I take a seat on the ground.

"Come sit, Jackson," he says. "You were always different when you were a little boy. You saw things differently from the other boys. You liked to paint and tell stories, just like me, just like your mum. And your art was always different, because you saw things other people didn't, and you expressed your art in a different way. I know you didn't always fit in. All I'm saying is we *are* connected, all of our people, even if sometimes you don't feel like it—we are all connected."

That fucking lump is returning to my throat.

"There's this shame," he continues. "It took our people by the throat long ago. If we don't let ourselves be who we are, love who we are, where we come from, it'll strangle ya until you can't fight it no longer. You know what I'm saying, Jackson?"

I nod. "I just don't know if I can do it," I say. "It's really hard sometimes."

"Jarny probably didn't help." Uncle Charlie smiles, placing his hand on my shoulder. "But you've probably hated yourself before, maybe for a long time. Maybe you still do. But those who love you, they love you no matter what. That's just how we are. We were all taught to love each other, unconditionally. One mob. All right?"

"All right," I say, but my voice quivers. "But can I still be connected? If I'm . . . you know?"

"There's nothing that can keep you from your culture, if you truly want it," Uncle Charlie whispers.

Then he stands, and I stand with him. He wraps his arms around me and we hug. It is the best hug I've had since Tomas left.

"Oh look," Uncle Charlie says, breaking from the hug and pointing to the lake. "Umbarra. Your totem."

A black duck swims across the lake. He's alone, just floating there.

"He's letting you know he's here to look after you."

I nearly giggle at the thought, but it's nice to see him floating there. Maybe he is actually looking out for me.

We join the rest of the group back at the bank. Uncle Charlie leaves with his grandson, and the other men start to leave. I finish the brown dots of my painting and plant it there behind the rock again. It's close to finished, but there's still some work to do.

Me, Jarny, and Kalyn set off across the lake on our canoes. The water is so clear beneath us that I can see the darkness of the lake's floor. The weeds and sunken branches show themselves in the deep.

On the other side of the lake, we can already hear the music playing from Troy's camp. We pull the canoes onto the sand and hide them in the bushes.

"Boys," Troy says at his campsite, greeting us with handshakes and half-hugs. "Our last hoorah. I'm sorry we got no beers left."

We take a seat with Troy and his father. Matt and Andy have left, and so has Jasmine. The night comes, and Levi waltzes over from his camp. I'm surprised to see he's still here. He blushes as Troy teases him for spewing up a few nights ago when they drank together.

This night is cooler than most recent nights. We move our chairs closer to the fire, because me, Jarny, and Kalyn are still just in our football shorts. I half expect Troy to bring up the whole situation of the photo he took of me and Tomas, or even just bring up how gay I am, but he doesn't say anything at all, or treat me any differently. He's just normal bogan Troy, which maybe isn't so bad.

Before long, Troy sneaks off with Jarny to the bushes to share a joint, after Kalyn and I refuse them. To be honest, I think getting high would just remind me of Tomas, and then I'd get sad and be all emotional about it.

"I'm heading home," Kalyn says to me with a yawn. "You coming?"

"Nah, all good. I might just sit by the fire for a bit," I say.

He leaves and it's just me and Levi there.

"Are you hungry?" Levi asks. "I think we got some leftover sausages and chops."

"Yeah," I reply, jumping to my feet. I follow Levi past Troy's fairy lights and through the camping ground. He uses his phone as a torch to guide our way.

We arrive at his camp and his parents are snoring in their tent. He opens a container and pulls out a plate wrapped in foil, peels the foil back, then hands me a sausage. It's cold and covered in hardened fat, but I eat it all. He hands me another, and we sit on the ground beside his dying campfire.

"Reckon youse will come back next year?" I ask, finishing off my second sausage.

"I'd say so," he says. "My mum really liked it. I kinda don't wanna leave."

"But you get to live in the city."

"Yeah, but I get sick of it." He finishes off his sausage and reaches over to drop the plate back inside the container. "It's nice to get away from the traffic and sirens, and planes going over your house every hour."

"Yeah? I dunno, just seems like there's this whole world out there that I haven't seen yet."

"That's how I feel about home too," he says, "until we go away again. Then it's like seeing a whole new country."

I turn and gaze upon Levi's face. His pale skin is turned orange and black by the night sky and the flickers of dying fire beside us. Our eyes meet and his face falls soft. He leans in, moving in slow motion. I lean in too. Our lips look for each other and come close enough to kiss. I do want to kiss him, but he's not Tomas.

"Sorry," I say. "I think I kind of have a boyfriend."

"Oh. Yeah, no worries." He smiles, and I smile back.

"I'll catch ya round, Levi. Maybe next year," I say as I stand. He stands with me.

"Yeah, maybe."

"Thanks for the food."

I walk back to Troy's camp. He and Jarny aren't back yet. The fire is burning out and the wood is just red coals now. The coals remind me of the end of the joint Tomas was smoking that night I came home late.

The coals remind me of Tomas.

The fire reminds me of Tomas.

The air reminds me of Tomas.

Then it all comes to me. I've figured it all out, just like that.

I head to the road. I walk fast up the mountain and onto the main street of the Mish. I don't stop even though my legs are burning, because I need to talk to him. I need to tell him.

I make it back home in no time. I tiptoe up the stairs and they creak with every step I take. I walk into my room and close the door, kick off my shoes, drop my pants, pull my shirt off my body, and throw it onto the growing pile under my window.

I fall onto my bed in my underwear and reach for my phone, which rests on my bedside table. I turn it on and find Aunty Pam's number.

Maybe he's asleep. Maybe he doesn't even want to talk to me, because he hasn't called me. Maybe I could drop my phone and sleep, but I need to tell him.

I dial Aunty Pam's number and put the phone to my ear. It rings and rings and rings, then there's an answer.

"Hello?" It's Aunty Pam's voice.

"Hey, Aunt," I say. "Sorry to call so late. Is Tomas there?"

She sighs. "Hold on."

I wait as the muffle of the phone drones and drones.

"Jackson?" Tomas asks. His voice sounds the same through the phone.

"Hey."

"Hey," he says. "Sorry I haven't called these past two weeks. I've just been busy with volunteering and lookin' after these kids and getting ready for court."

"That's okay. I'm sorry too."

There's quiet for a moment. I can feel my heart beating through my whole body.

"I need to tell you something," I say, almost whispering. My voice quivers.

"What?"

"I'm gonna try to enroll back in school," I say.

"That's great. Good for you."

"And . . ." I take a deep breath and swallow. "I'm gay." The world fades from my chest and I feel like a whole person for the first time in I don't know how long. "I also wanted to tell you that I'm gay."

Tomas chuckles on the other end of the line. "I'm happy for you," he says. "Can I let you in on a secret?"

"Yeah," I say.

"So am I," he whispers. "I'm gay as fuck."

I focus on the cushioning of my bed against my back as the smile grows stronger on my face and the tears race to my eyes. I listen to his breaths as they come to my ear. I feel different through my whole body, like I've become not just a whole person but a new person. We stay quiet for a moment.

"I don't know if it's just relief, but I think I'm ready to tell my mum," I say.

"Yeah?"

"Yeah. I might be."

I hear his smile through his breaths. "That's great. I'm glad."

"What about you?" I ask.

"Yeah, maybe," he says.

Maybe we can do it together on the same day. I smile at the thought and close my eyes.

"I missed your voice," I say. My eyelids are heavy.

"I missed yours too."

We're quiet for another moment. I don't mind the silence, because I know he is still there.

"You know what," he says. "I actually wrote another story for a comic book . . ."

"Don't you mean *graphic novel?*" I tease.

He snickers. "Yeah, whatever. But I wrote the story, and I did some of the sketches, but I was thinking you could redraw them since you're a better drawer? If you want to, I mean. You don't have to."

"Yeah," I say, "I'll do it. Just mail them to me."

"You sure?"

"Yes, I'm sure." I wonder if he's smiling as widely as I am.

"Oh, by the way," he says. "I saw this ad on TV, for this new show called *Cleverman.*"

"*Cleverman?*"

"Yeah. It's about this Aboriginal superhero," he giggles.

"Damn. They beat us to it."

His voice sounds a little different. Maybe I'm just tired. All I know is I'm glad to be talking to Tomas again.

TWENTY-FOUR

Another week has gone by, and now I'm sitting with Mum at the desk in the principal's office. Mum wipes the sweat from her brow, fanning herself with my folded enrollment papers.

"What the hell's takin' 'em so long?" she asks, with a sharpness to her voice.

"Mum, you need to chill out."

The door opens behind us and the principal, Mr. Truman, walks in. He's shaved his famous Tom Selleck mustache. Maybe he's having a midlife crisis or something. Following him into the office is Susan, the school counselor. She gives us a smile as she sits in the chair beside me. Last through the door is Michael, the Aboriginal Liaison. He wears a black shirt with Aboriginal designs on it and stands to the side of the principal's desk, folding his arms.

"Sorry for the delay," Mr. Truman says.

"Don't you mob have any funding for air conditioners?" Mum snaps.

"Mum," I interrupt, placing my casted hand on her forearm.

"Sorry, Kris," Mr. Truman says. "Actually, our funding is pretty tight at the moment. Unfortunately, we don't get as much money as the private schools." He turns to me. "But I'm pleased to hear Jackson wants to return to school to do Year Twelve. There's just the issue of the assault charges . . ."

"The court threw them out," Mum says. "Judge said Jackson was defending himself."

"I'm pleased to hear his charges were dismissed," Mr. Truman says, forcing a smile onto his face. He turns to me. "Despite that, it's possible some of the parents might be concerned that if we let you come back to school, you might put the other students in danger."

"That whitefella called him an *abo*. Of course he punched him. I'd be disappointed if he hadn't," Mum says, which brings a smile to the corner of my mouth.

"Whatever the case, I think the best course of action would be for us to put in place some strict rules for Jackson, as well as some strong supports. This would help erase any worries the parents' committee might have." Mr. Truman shifts his gaze to Susan. "Jackson, you know Susan?"

"Yeah."

"I'm glad you're coming back, Jackson," Susan says. "Just following on from what Mr. Truman said, we want to make sure we're giving you some strong supports while you're here, so that we can keep you on track with your schoolwork and keep the other students safe. Not that we think you're dangerous, but as a school, when one of our students has an incident like yours, we want to make sure we do everything we can to help. So, what I'd like is for us to have a session each Friday afternoon and Monday morning. Just half an hour, doesn't have to be long. Does that sound okay to you?"

I nod. "Yeah, that's fine."

"And I'll be checking in on you," Michael jumps in. "You know where my office is, so you can come and see me whenever you need, or if someone says something to you in class and you get angry, or even if you just feel like you can't sit in the classroom. Just come to my office and we'll have an apple or something."

I nod and I realize I'm not forcing the smile onto my face. "Sounds good," I say.

"Well, Jackson," Mr. Truman says as he stands, "we look forward to having you back when we start on Tuesday. Bring those enrollment forms with you, yeah?"

"Thanks," I say as I shake his hand, and as I shake Michael's and Susan's hands.

I follow Mum back through the corridors, which are lined with lockers. We walk out to the car park and load into the Toyota Camry Mum impulsively bought a few days ago with the money she got from selling some of her old paintings.

We get back on the road, kept cool by the icy air-con of Mum's new car. We head for the Mish but get held up by some road-work on the highway. Ahead, they are re-tarring the road. I spot some of the workers just hanging out in their vests, resting by a truck in the shade. I realize one of the lazy workers is Ethan. His red beard is looking thicker, and he's all sweaty. As we begin to move along the road, I feel the urge to wind down the window and shout something at him. *Racist dog* comes to mind. But

I don't bother. I might strain my voice if I yell, and it is really not worth it.

"I'm glad you decided to go back to school," Mum says as we park the car at home. "And I'm glad we still have two hours before Henry gets dropped off by the Walkers!"

I follow her inside and pour us both a glass of orange juice. She starts one of her Charley Pride CDs, skipping through the songs until she comes to "Kiss an Angel Good Mornin'." She hums along for a moment.

"Sit with me," she says, taking a seat at the kitchen table. It kind of feels like this would be a perfect moment to come out to her, but I'm not sure I'm ready yet.

I sit opposite her and sip from my glass of juice.

"You know," she says, "when I was a kid, there wasn't a chance any of us blackfellas would finish school. Most of us only went to Year Nine or Ten. But you kids these days have so many opportunities we didn't."

"I know, Mum." I smile.

"I just want you to know how proud I am of you for deciding to finish Year Twelve. It was a very mature decision."

She starts fanning herself again with my enrollment papers. She's quiet for a moment as we listen to the music.

"Have you talked to Tomas since he left?" she asks.

"Yeah, a few times."

"Just a *few* times?" She fans herself faster, and I can feel the wind from across the table.

"Yeah, he'll get sick of me if I just keep ringing and ringing."

I sense something inside her as she stares at me. "You should call him," she says.

"Now?"

"I think he'd like to know that you're going back to school, wouldn't he?"

"I don't know." I finish my glass of juice and notice the ring I've made on the wooden table surface. "Maybe he'd want to know, maybe not."

She studies my face. I just smile and look away.

"I think you should give him a call," she says. She stands and leaves for the backyard. I pull my phone from my pocket and text Aunty Pam.

Can you tell Tomas I got accepted back at school? Love ya xo

I head to the sink and rinse my glass. Mum's setting up her easel outside, humming along to the music. She places her fresh blank canvas on the easel and sits on her painting stool.

My phone vibrates in my hand. It's a message from Kalyn.

Come for pre-drinks.

I'd forgotten about the party tonight. I race upstairs and change into my jeans and shirt. Then I head back down to the backyard, where Mum is now painting her canvas brown.

"I'm off to Kalyn's," I say.

"All right. Well, stay outta trouble. Don't be out too late."

I walk out of the house and make my way along the main street of the Mish. I arrive at Kalyn's and walk through his back gate. He's sitting at his outdoor table with Jarny. There's a carton of beers beside them, and I take a bottle as I sit down.

"They lettin' me back in," I announce.

"Good. Now they'll have *three* choices for the acknowledgment of country," Kalyn says. We chuckle and I drink my beer.

"What's Tommy been up to?" Jarny asks.

"Dunno, he's been writing and stuff," I say, taking a sip from my beer.

"You haven't talked to him?"

"Yeah, a few times." I take a bigger sip from my beer.

"Just *a few times*? But you like him, don't you?" Jarny asks, leaning forward and resting his elbows against the table. He's sounding a bit like Mum.

"Yeah," I say. I realize I'm blushing, so I pretend to scratch my eye and cover my cheek. "But I dunno. It's weird to think about *dating* a guy, isn't it?"

"Why is it weird?" Jarny's teasing me now.

"Because . . . I dunno. It's just . . . different. And if I'm calling all the time, he'll probably get sick of me."

"He won't get sick of you," Kalyn chimes in. "Be good to just keep in touch."

"Yeah, I guess."

"Otherwise, that Jasper guy is coming tonight. You remember him from bio last year?" Jarny asks.

I remember him from bio, and I remember him from the medical center when Bobby got bitten by the snake, and Kalyn said that thing about the shampoo bottle.

"I know for sure he's gay," Jarny continues. "I could set youse up if you want?"

I nearly choke on my drink.

"God. No, please don't," I say. We all laugh, and I finish my beer in one more big sip.

I can't help but think about Tomas as Kalyn and Jarny start talking with each other. I wonder what he's doing. Maybe he's got court soon. Maybe he's going to court tomorrow. Maybe he's already been, or maybe he's at someone's house just like I am, getting ready for a party of his own.

Night begins to fall around eight o'clock. The chatter of the nearing guests grows louder as they make their way along the main street of the Mish. They must be already drunk. They come through Kalyn's back gate. Abby leads them, with Tesha behind her and two other girls following.

Tesha comes over and props her bottle of Passion Pop on the table. She sits at the table with us, and Abby sits on her lap. Tesha avoids looking at me, I notice. I don't think she knows about me and Tomas yet.

We get drunk together, and a car pulls up out front. It's some of the white kids from school. They all shake my hand and tell me how happy they are that I'm coming back to do Year 12. Word travels fast, clearly.

By ten o'clock, I'm still at the table, and it seems most of the white kids in our grade last year are in Kalyn's backyard, drinking with us. As I glance over their faces, I spot Tesha coming towards me.

"Congrats," she says, sitting down. "It's good you're going back to school."

"Thanks. You're not going back, eh?"

"Nah, gonna go to TAFE, so I can get a job quicker."

It's awkward. We haven't really spoken since I told her I didn't love her. I wonder whether she hates me for it.

My phone vibrates in my pocket. I pull it out and there's a message from Aunty Pam.

Just told Tomas you're enrolled again. He said he's happy to hear. Love ya 2 xo.

Jarny comes over to me while a group of white kids start setting up cups on the table for a game of beer pong. He staggers a little, and I almost have to catch him when he arrives to sit next to me.

"Jackson," he begins, "I love you, man."

I just laugh.

"Love you too." I take a sip from the beer I'm holding while Jarny swings his arm around my shoulders.

"Jasper's here."

I choke on my drink. "Who?"

"You know? *Jasper . . .*"

He is so fucking drunk. I want to punch him to sleep. My heart's beginning to race. He just cuddles in close to me and points across the backyard. Yep. It is definitely Jasper. He's wearing a blue T-shirt and jeans, with thin glasses over his eyes. He is cute, sure, but I don't care. Jarny is about to give me away.

"That's great, cuz," I say, before standing up to make an escape. "I gotta piss."

I zoom inside at speed. I find my way to the bathroom and splash my face with water from the bathroom sink, realizing how drunk I am. I can still walk straight and talk properly, but I am definitely drunk. And in some part of me, I'm feeling adventurous. In some distant part of me, it almost feels like the right thing, for Jarny to *out* me to everyone. Like ripping off a Band-Aid—it would be done, and then I wouldn't have to *come out* myself.

That's how I know I'm drunk, because I am beginning to consider talking to Jasper. I try to imagine it. I doubt any of the white kids would care. They might be surprised, but they probably wouldn't care. Maybe Jasper wouldn't even be interested in me. Maybe he would never even consider me. Maybe he thinks I'm ugly. Maybe I'm not his type. Maybe he doesn't like boys at all and we all just assumed he was gay because he *looks* gay sometimes.

I stay in the bathroom for so long, staring at myself in the mirror. My face is still wet, so I dry it with a nearby hand towel.

There's a bang at the door, so I leave the bathroom, passing the girl busting to go on my way out. I don't even know who she is.

Back outside, Jarny is on all fours beside Kalyn on the grass. There's some fresh vomit next to him and Kalyn rubs his back. The music has been dulled, and a group of white people are leaving.

As I watch Jarny being comforted by Kalyn while he lets out another vomit, my mind drifts back to Tomas. I remember the care he showed me; how good he made me feel when he took me in his arms. I remember feeling so confused and angry and ashamed, and how easy it was for him to take all of that away with just a kiss. I can feel it coming, a good old cry. I shake my head and rid myself of it. I down the rest of my beer and go inside for another.

Tesha finds me beside the fridge inside the house. "What was that about before?"

"What?"

"With Jarny?"

She was listening, at the table. I shrug and shake my head. "I dunno. I think he was confused. He's pretty drunk."

"Yeah, true," Tesha says with a little laugh.

Maybe she knows. Maybe Kalyn told her, even though he said he wouldn't tell anyone. Maybe she just wants me to admit it to her.

"Me and Abby are going back to her place for a few drinks," she says. "Do you wanna come?"

I almost say yes. But I can't. I'm too drunk, and there are things I need to say. I take her hand and lead her through the people gathered inside Kalyn's house. We walk out the front door and onto the porch. I sit on the steps leading down to the front lawn and Tesha sits beside me. There is a smell of cigarette smoke in the air, but no one else is out here.

"I need to tell you something," I begin. That nervous ball has returned to my stomach again. "When I said I don't love you, I didn't mean I don't care about you. And it wasn't because I don't like you, because I do!"

Tesha nods along, but I can tell she's confused.

"The truth is I really do like you, as a person. And I like you as a friend too."

"Uh, okay."

I shake my head. I've always been so bad at saying what I want to say.

"I'm just gonna say it." I look her in the eyes. I open my mouth, but I'm almost choking on air. "I . . . I . . ."

"You what?" she asks, nearing laughter, but her voice is soft. "It's all right."

"I don't really . . . like . . . girls . . ."

There's silence for a moment. The whole world could be listening to us. Her eyebrows climb to the top of her forehead, and I have to look away. I want to run as far away as possible.

"Okay," she begins, but just then Abby bangs through the front door, and in turning to see her, I notice someone else is standing in the dark at the other end of the porch. A few of the boys and girls from school follow Abby as she grabs Tesha's arm.

"There you are," she shouts at Tesha. "Let's get."

Abby yanks Tesha to her feet and pulls her onto the lawn. Tesha looks back to me with a smile as they head out the gate and start down the road. I just stay there, my ass planted on the porch in uncertainty.

I can smell the person smoking in the dark. Tears threaten to come to my eyes. *I shouldn't have told her, not while I'm drunk.* "Can I bum a ciggie?" I ask the stranger.

The figure goes for their pocket, takes out a packet, walks out of the dark, and it is Jasper. His black shoes click on the wooden porch. He hands his cigarettes to me and I take one.

"That was pretty awkward," he whispers with a smile on his face. "Have you told many people?"

"Just a few."

"Do you feel better after?"

"I feel annoyed."

He chuckles. I chuckle too.

"Yeah, it can be pretty annoying, having to tell people," he says as he sits beside me. "There shouldn't be any need for *coming out.*"

He smells nice. Through the smoke, I can smell his deodorant.

Maybe he's just sweating hard, and it's made the deodorant more active, but he smells good.

"Why are you out here by yourself?" I ask.

"None of my friends smoke, so I thought I'd come out here so no one has to smell it."

"Oh. Yeah, I don't smoke either," I say. I hand back the cigarette Jasper gave me, while he laughs to himself.

"Someone said you're coming back to school?"

"Yeah. They didn't really wanna let me back. I had a bit of trouble with the cops a few weeks ago."

"So, you're a *bad boy*?" he teases. His voice is soft and calming. It floats in the air when he speaks.

"Not really," I reply. Oh, god, I remember Jarny wanting to set me up with this guy, and now here he is, strangely meeting me in the dark on the porch. "Did Jarny talk to you?" I ask.

"Jarny? Nah, Kalyn invited me."

"I mean, did he talk to you about me?"

"I don't think so. Why's that?"

"Don't worry, it's nothing." My head is spinning, and I feel a bit sick. "Yeah. I should probably go home."

"It's not even eleven yet!"

"I know." I smile.

Jasper studies me as we share a moment of staring at each other. "You sure you'll make it back?" he teases.

I just smile. "Yeah, it's, like, just down the road. Literally."

I stumble down the stairs and fall onto the lawn. "Fuck," I whisper to myself. My hand is stinging in its cast. Jasper helps me to my feet.

"Thanks," I mutter.

"I'll walk you home."

"No, I don't want to ruin your night."

"You won't. I'm getting picked up soon, anyway."

His grip on my arm is gentle as he holds me up. His eyes are brown under the moonlight, just like Tomas's. I nod, and we walk out of the front yard together.

Jasper's quiet as we make our way along the road. I worry that he's going to try to come inside my house and into my room. I worry he's going to try to have sex with me.

"I thought you just lived down the road?" Jasper fakes a tired voice.

"I do!"

The stars are few in the sky and the air is starting to cool. We pass the community center and the streetlight and arrive in front of my house.

"This is me," I say.

"Do you want me to help you inside?" he asks.

"No, don't bother. I'm . . . I'm too drunk to . . . umm . . . Besides, my mum and brother will probably be awake, and they don't know I'm . . . you know?"

"What? Oh, no, no, you got the wrong idea, man . . ."

I want to slap myself as the blush rushes back to my cheeks.

"Shit, I'm sorry."

"I just don't want you to fall over and hurt yourself." Jasper laughs.

I feel so stupid. "Of course," I say. "You're just being nice."

"Are you always this awkward?" he jokes with a smile.

I try to shake the embarrassment from myself and walk through the front gate. I close it behind me and hold my hands there for a moment.

"I mean, I would . . . If I could . . . I would invite you in . . . but I think I kind of have a boyfriend. *Kind of.*"

I never say things like that. It's the fucking alcohol.

"Well, if you had asked, and you were *kind of* single, I might've said yes. Who knows?" he says with a cheeky smile, just like the one Tomas used to give me.

There's silence for a moment, then we both laugh.

"I guess I'll see you at school," he says.

"Yeah. I'll say *hey* when I see you."

He smiles a smile that shows he's just as embarrassed for me as I am. He's still there when I make it to the front door, so I give him a wave and he returns it, then I walk inside. All my energy rushes back through my blood, and I race up my stairs, hook my phone to the charger. It powers on and I ring Aunty Pam's number.

"Hello?" she answers.

I sit down on the side of my bed. "Hey, Aunt, it's Jackson."

"Jackson, you gotta stop ringing me so late."

"Sorry, Aunt."

"You looking for Tomas? I just got him a new phone. I'll text you his number."

"Oh. All right, great!"

"Okay. Love you, Neph. Bye."

I watch my phone screen for what feels like hours. Finally, a text comes with Tomas's number. I ring it. It rings and rings and rings. It goes to voice mail and I hang up. A text comes through from Tomas: *Who's this?*

I text back: *Jackson, ya fool.*

My phone starts to ring and I answer. I'm nearly out of breath from the anticipation.

"Hey," I say.

"Are you drunk?" Tomas asks playfully. "I was gonna call you tomorrow. Aunty Pam just got me this phone earlier. It's just a cheap one, but it's fine."

"That's all right. I'm sorry I haven't really called. But I realized something just before."

"What's that?"

"We aren't really a *couple* or anything, like we aren't together, like a *couple*, you know? We never talked about anything like that."

"Okay,"

"But what I'm saying is I would . . . I would like to be . . . like . . . a couple . . . with you . . . if you wanted to be . . ."

"Be a couple? Like boyfriends?"

"Yes. That's exactly what I'm asking. I'm asking if you'll be my boyfriend."

I'm breathless again and my stomach is in knots as I sit on my bedside.

"Like, a real couple?" he asks.

"Yes," I say. "I want to hold your hand and walk along the beach with you. I want to buy you presents and take you for a picnic on Valentine's Day. I want to be your boyfriend." I hear Tomas sniffling. "Only if you want to be mine too. I know it'll be hard, with the distance and all, but—"

"I want to," Tomas interrupts. "But you know what that means? We'll have to . . . *come out*, won't we?"

"Maybe. Maybe we don't have to do anything," I say. "Besides, I don't feel so scared about that anymore."

I unhook my phone and rest back against my mattress. We are quiet. I can hear Tomas breathing through the phone. He sniffles again, and I find something inside me. It pushes the horror aside and makes me feel taller, stronger.

"I mean, if we do need to *come out*, then I think I'm ready," I say. "I'm ready if you are."

"You're ready?"

"Yeah, I think so. We can do it together, when the time comes. Then my mum will know and Aunty Pam will know and there won't be any secret anymore."

"Slow down," Tomas laughs.

"There's just nothing I want more right now." A tear escapes from my eye.

"Maybe not just yet," he says. "I don't think I'm all the way ready to come out yet. Maybe I will be soon. I dunno."

"That's okay. There's no rush."

I stand and walk to my bedroom window. The cooling night breeze finds its way inside. I let it blow against me as I stand there in the dark.

"Will you still be my boyfriend, though?" Tomas asks.

"Yes, *obviously.*"

I sit back on my bed and we talk for a while. When we finally hang up, I'm all out of energy. The thought of coming out makes me nervous, but not in a *bad* way anymore. Before, it would have scared me into a hole in the ground or even inside myself, and I would have probably never crawled back out, but it doesn't scare me so much now, knowing me and Tomas will do it together; knowing my friends have my back.

I feel stronger as I rest my head on my pillow. Nothing can hurt me. Maybe I am ready. Maybe I'm truly ready. Maybe. One thing I'm sure of, though, is that I just can't wait to wake up tomorrow—so I can call my boyfriend and tell him I love him.

This book is informed by my own experience of growing up in a small country town in New South Wales as part of a big Aboriginal family. This story deals with a number of important themes and issues relevant to First Australians, all of which have informed the writing choices I've made.

Racism is very prevalent towards First Nations people in Australian society (you just need to read the comments sections of social media posts regarding any First Nations issue to see it) and therefore is prevalent in this book.

Jackson is a creation of my imagination. The character of Tomas is also a creation of my imagination, and while life has brought me experience working with Aboriginal youth in the out-of-home care system and youth justice system, Tomas is not based on any real person. While Tomas is fictional, many of the issues he faces are real and have informed my writing. I encourage you as the reader to do your own research on these issues.

The Mish and its neighboring town, while minimally inspired by a combination of real places, are both fictional creations for the purposes of the story. The characters who live there and the activities that take place on the Mish in this story are all fictitious and should not be taken to reflect the experiences of all people living in Aboriginal communities in New South Wales.

This book explores the singular experience of one Aboriginal boy and his journey to accepting his sexuality and finding his place in the world. While Jackson's experience mirrors my own in a number of ways, his life as depicted in the story should not be taken as a complete reflection of my own. Jackson's and my experiences will differ from the experiences of other First Nations Australian people who identify as LGBTQIA+. Having said that, one of the reasons I wrote this book is because I hadn't come across any young adult stories centered around an Aboriginal teen coming to terms with their sexuality and accepting who they are. I'd like to think reading this book as a teen myself might have helped me on my journey, and I hope soon there will be many, many more books like this for Aboriginal and Torres Strait Islander teens—and other First Nations teens across the world—to read.

Acknowledgments

This book is the result of over two years of hard work and a lot of helping hands along the way. I could write forty pages of thank-yous, but I'll try to keep it short and sweet.

I'd firstly like to thank Jodie Webster and Elise Jones of Allen & Unwin, who made my first time through the publishing process so exciting, meaningful, and fun. A million thanks to the rest of the crew at Allen & Unwin for all your hard work on my book, including Jennifer Castles for her extremely valuable feedback and support, and for championing my book from the very beginning.

I take great pleasure in thanking many teachers who have shown great support to me and my writing during my school years and beyond. A special thanks to the teachers of St. Pat's Primary School in Bega, especially my Year 6 teacher, Maureen Scott, who asked twelve-year-old me to send her a copy of my first book. Special thanks to the teachers of Bega High School, especially my Year 12 English teacher, Greg Bartlett, for always cheering on my writing, and my year advisor, Douglas Whitaker, who has continuously supported me through my teen years and into adulthood. Thank you to all the Aboriginal education officers I've been supported by during my school years.

I also need to thank my very special personal support group—fellow writers Gabbie Stroud and Kate Liston-Mills—who have championed and challenged me from day one. I'm so thankful to have you both in my corner. I extend this thanks to all my workmates and friends who have supported my writing journey and especially those who read my crappy early drafts. I'm sure I will forget someone, so I won't name you all here, but know I am forever thankful.

I must thank my massive family—my cousins, aunts, uncles, and grandparents. I hope you love this book as much as I do. I thank my brothers, Ryan, Lochlan, and Damon, and I need to give an extra-special thanks to my extraordinary sister, Hayleigh. Thank you for letting me rant all my ideas at you late at night. Thank you for reading everything I've ever written and for being my biggest fan.

Finally, I thank my Mum and Dad—the strongest characters I'll ever know in my life, who always taught me to be proud of who I am. I owe this book to you both.

About the Author

Gary Lonesborough is a Yuin man who grew up on the Far South Coast of New South Wales as part of a large and proud Aboriginal family. Growing up a massive Kylie Minogue and North Queensland Cowboys fan, Gary was always writing as a child and continued his creative journey when he moved to Sydney to study at film school. Gary has experience working in Aboriginal health, the disability sector (including experience working in the youth justice system), and the film industry. He was Bega Valley Shire Council Young Citizen of the Year, won the Patrick White Young Indigenous Writers Award, and has received a Copyright Agency First Nations Fellowship. *Ready When You Are* (published in Australia as *The Boy from the Mish*) is Gary's debut YA novel.